A Gangster's Revenge 4

Aryanna

Lock Down Publications
Presents
A Gangster's Revenge 4
A Novel by *Aryanna*

Aryanna

Lock Down Publications

P.O. Box 1482

Pine Lake, Ga 30072-1482

Visit our website at **www.lockdownpublications.com**

Lock Down Publications
Like our page on Facebook: Lock Down Publications
@www.facebook.com/lockdownpublications.ldp
Cover design and layout by: Dynasty's Cover Me
Book interior design by: Shawn Walker
Edited by: Lauren Burton

Aryanna

Acknowledgments

Father God, you've brought me this far, and so it's you that I thank first always. I give many, many thanks to my beautiful Belinda Diane for all that you do and all that you endure. Everything doesn't begin to describe what you are to me. I have to thank my fans that rock with me through it all. You've helped me make my dreams come true, and I can't put into words how much that means to me. I have to acknowledge and thank my girl Reds Johnson – you saw me even when I was in the dark. You acknowledged me when you didn't have to. I want you to know that I carry your words with me as inspiration, because they mean something. We family 4 lyfe! Now, let's get this collaboration done! LOL! I have to thank all of my family and friends who support me. I have to thank all my niggas stuck behind enemy lines that provide both inspiration and comic relief. I have to thank my beautiful kids: Micaela, Izzy, and Aryanna. Who am I without you? It's my goal to change the game for you and give you everything I never had. The Game Is Ours!

Aryanna

Dedication

This book is dedicated to everyone I've lost, especially my Pops, Douglas Terry Evans. I hope all of you are watching over me, because I need your guidance.

Aryanna

Chapter One

Brianna

2040

The world moved around me like the faint hum of a car's engine, but I was oblivious to the hustle and bustle. A child's cries of pain, a mother's wail for mercy, all fell on deaf ears as I continued looking at the dried blood that stained my hands. So much blood, and in the end what did it all mean? What was all the death and destruction for?

Everyone had their reason and justifications, but when the smoke cleared, here were the facts: tonight's actions had changed everybody's lives forever, including my own. The man I'd loved for longer than I could remember was fighting for his life, and the harsh reality was until he was dead, he'd always be fighting for it.

And what of the other man who'd worked his way into my heart by complete accident? Was I supposed to forget him and give him over to what fate had in store? How could I possibly do that without a lifetime of regrets and *what-ifs* haunting me? The reality I was faced with was there were no easy decisions, because if there were, then everyone would be a part of this lifestyle. Every sucka would claim to be a gangsta, and every bitch would swear she deserved to be queen.

I'd been around long enough to know nothing came to a sleeper except a dream, so if I wanted something I'd better wake my ass up and go get it. I knew this was my alarm clock going off. The task in front of me was daunting, though, because my desire was for something different than the money, power, respect, and revenge that caused so much havoc. I wanted the unthinkable. I wanted peace.

"Bri!" I heard her yell, snatching my focus away from the answers I sought between my blood-caked fingers.

"Ms. Gladys," I said, rising and wrapping my arms around her tiny frame despite all the blood covering my clothing. "Baby, what happened?" she asked, pulling back and searching my face for answers destined to break her heart.

I felt a fresh trickle of tears escape my sore eyes, following the same beaten path as their predecessors, as my mind went backward three hours to another world. It was on the tip of my tongue to tell her everything without sparing any detail, but in order for my plan to work, a secret had to go to the grave.

"Devaughn came to the house looking for DJ, but he wasn't there. I made him bring me with him to look for him, and we ended up here, but it was Devonte we saw first. They argued, but I stood in between them so they couldn't shoot each other. Then– then DJ showed up, and Devaughn tried to stop him from shooting Tae. I don't know what happened. It was like I blinked and everybody started shooting."

"Did Tae…? Is he…?"

"Him and DJ both have been in surgery for the past three hours. They both lost a lot of blood, even though they were in surgery moments after the shooting. DJ was hit twice in the chest, once above the heart and once dead center. And Tae, I overheard the doctor say something about him being hit and his lungs filled up with blood."

"Oh God," she murmured, almost collapsing in my arms. I felt her pain in more ways than one, but I couldn't break down right then because the next few hours would be crucial to everyone's future.

"I bet, since the police were called, my coward of a son disappeared into the night while his children fight for their lives, huh? No good son of a bi—."

"He's dead," I whispered, not knowing how she'd take the news, given their estrangement, but not wanting her to put her foot any further in her mouth.

"Dead? Impossible. He can't die."

I didn't really know what to say as I watched this woman I loved and respected battle love and hate within herself. I had no idea what had ultimately caused them to live as if the other was dead, but as a mother myself, I knew it didn't matter because he was still her child.

"Dead? But how?"

"Caught in the crossfire."

"Who shot him?"

"I don't know, Ms. Gladys."

My response caused her to look at me, really look at me, in search of the truth that lay hidden within.

"You don't know? But you were here, Brianna. You saw the whole goddamn thing!"

"It all happened so fast, and—"

"Ms. Gladys?"

We both turned to see a petite, light-skinned nurse walking toward us. I recognized her immediately as the first one who got to Devonte after he was shot.

"How are they, Tiffany?" Ms. Gladys asked quickly.

"They're both in stable condition and sedated. No disrespect, Ms. Gladys, but what the fuck is going on? These are Devaughn's sons? And he got caught in the middle?"

"It's a long story, baby. Just tell me my grandsons will be alright."

"Oh, they'll survive this round, but what difference will it make when they seem determined to kill each other?"

"I know, I just need to get Devonte out of here as soon as possible and—"

"That's not gonna stop it," I said, catching the look Tiffany threw my way as if I'd spoke out of turn.

"And you are?" she asked in a tone that said she wanted to roll her neck.

"Devonte is the father of my child."

"So then, why were you—"

"Stay focused and listen for a second," I interjected before she could spill any info about how I'd come unglued when DJ got shot. "Taking Tae to New York won't fix anything. There is only one way to end this thing for good."

"And what's that?" Ms. Gladys asked.

"We have to convince everyone Devonte is dead. It's the only way the war ends, and it's the only way DJ won't hunt him to the ends of the Earth."

I could see Ms. Gladys giving my words careful contemplation, but I had no doubt she would arrive at the exact same conclusion. Were my motivations selfish? In a way, yes, because choosing between the man I thought I knew and the man I wanted to know was impossible. Love was blind for a reason, and I had no intention of asking myself the hard questions right now. Shit, I was amazed to be still holding it together!

"Can it be done, Tiff?" she asked, her gaze darting around the E.R. to see who was paying attention to our conversation.

"It's gonna cost," Tiffany replied, staring at me with blatant distrust in her brown eyes.

She was only 5'0" if that, weighing a scary 110 pounds, so I was confident I could smash her if that was what it came down to. For the moment I just gave her that universal *bitch, this ain't what you want* look, to which she smiled mischievously in response.

"Money ain't a problem. Will you get it done, Tiff?"

14

"Anything for you, Ms. Gladys. This is my family, too. Give me some time to put everything into play, and just sit out here and look distraught."

"That won't be hard," she replied huskily, wiping tears from her tired brown eyes.

I knew she was up there in years, but at that moment she looked a few days past a hundred, and it broke my heart to see her that way. The two women hugged, and then Tiffany retreated the way she'd come, leaving us alone again.

"Brianna, I want you to tell me what exactly happened from the time Devaughn ran into Devonte."

"Okay, so—"

"Where's my father?"

Neither of us had seen the woman approach, but we both knew exactly who she was, and the mean-looking pistol she was holding by her side made it clear what was on her mind.

Aryanna

Chapter Two

Deshana

I couldn't shake the feeling in the pit of my stomach since I'd gotten the call from Belinda. She didn't explain how my father knew what was going on, but it didn't matter, because having him on the front line was not what I wanted. The conscious decision to go against his wishes was contrary to my nature because I loved and respected my father, but I knew the torment DJ felt to some degree.

When my own mother had been kidnapped, I saw all types of visions of her death play on the back of my eyelids until she was safe again. The pain I felt just imagining the possibilities paled in comparison to what DJ had to live with, and for that reason I understood his thirst for revenge. That understanding didn't stop the doom tingling my nerve endings, or wipe away the beads of sweat lining my upper lip.

"Slow down, babe," JuJu cautioned as I cut in front of an eighteen-wheeler and fish-tailed my silver 2041 E Class Benz up the hospital exit ramp.

"I got to get there before my Pops does," I responded, stomping the gas pedal as far as it would go.

"I understand that, but if we get in an accident or get pulled over, we're gonna have to explain the naked bitch in the trunk."

I knew she was right, but I didn't care. I was determined to get to my destination, and anyone who got in the way could have one of my bullets as a souvenir.

I knew DJ was a hothead, so getting into a shootout with Tae in the middle of a hospital was just his style. My only hope was that our father could reason with him. I slid to a stop in front of the E.R. entrance, immediately spotting my father's Porsche 911 and DJ's Bugatti parked side-by-side a few feet away.

"Stay in the car," I told JuJu.

Pulling my black, wood-handled Colt .45, I stepped out and made my way inside. With my pistol pressed to my leg for concealment, I scanned the halls, looking for my family and any enemies simultaneously while staying alert for any cops. The good news was I didn't see anyone fitting the bill of law enforcement. The bad news was I could smell gun smoke in the air.

I expected to smell blood and death in a hospital, but gun smoke was as out of place as a stripper pole. I rounded the corner to find Brianna huddled next to a woman I hadn't laid eyes on in thirteen years, but the slump of her shoulders told me this wasn't the family reunion anyone envisioned.

"Where's my father?" I asked without preamble. The look on both their faces showed my presence had taken them by surprise, but the panic flooding my grandmother's eyes made my stomach drop to my knees.

"Where's my father?"

"Put – put your gun away, Deshana. The cops could be still lurking," my grandmother advised.

"What happened, and where the fuck is my father?" I asked more forcefully, tightening my grip on my pistol.

"He's—"

"Who's here for Devonte Briggs?" a slender brunette asked, coming through the operating room doors directly behind the front desk.

"We are," my grandmother responded, stepping directly in front of me.

I took this opportunity to push my gun down into the waist of my jeans, but I really wanted to shoot the next muthafucka who didn't answer my question.

"I'm Doctor McKenna, the on-duty surgeon."

"How is he, Doctor?"

"Ma'am, I'm sorry, but – but we lost him. I did everything I could, but the internal bleeding was too severe. I'm sorry for your loss," she said, taking my grandmother's hand and squeezing it.

I saw her shoulders shaking, indicating she was crying, but I felt nothing. We may have been siblings, but I didn't know him nor care about him. My only consolation was with his death and our takeover of New York, this war would once and for all be over.

"Is Devaughn Mitchell Jr. awake yet?" Brianna asked.

"He—"

"What the fuck happened to DJ?" I demanded, pushing Brianna aside so I could address the Doctor personally.

"Ma'am, who are you to the patient?" she asked calmly.

"I'm his sister, now tell me what the fuck happened!"

"He was shot twice in the chest, but we successfully removed both bullets and stopped the bleeding."

"He's alive?"

"Luckily, yes. He's still recovering from surgery, and it'll be a little while before you can see him."

"Is our father with him now?"

"Your father?" she repeated, looking at first my grandmother and then Brianna before her gaze returned to mine.

"Ma'am, he—"

"Thank you, Doctor," my grandmother said, again squeezing her hand.

The Doctor retreated the way she'd come, and my grandmother turned to face me. The words she was trying to formulate telegraphed themselves to me before she opened her mouth, and I knew. Truthfully, I'd already known because I was my daddy's baby, even at thirty-six years old. There was only one question remaining.

"Who killed him?"

I could now see that same question mirrored in my grandmother's eyes, which caused us both to turn toward a nervous and fidgety Brianna.

"I asked a question, little girl," I reminded her, stepping a little closer so she could get a whiff of the barely containable fury within me.

"It was – it was Tae. He shot him in the head while trying to kill DJ."

"And DJ killed him?"

"Yeah!" she murmured with tears in her eyes.

I didn't know what to say, didn't even know what to feel aside from guilt and rage. Guilt because I should've never gone against my father's wishes, and if I hadn't he'd be alive right then. His death was on me, on my hands, even though I hadn't pulled the trigger. And the rage. The rage I couldn't put into words, but I'd damn sure put it into action for the rest of my life.

It was time to finish what I and my daddy had started so long ago, and I'd let the world feel my rage!

"So, your baby daddy killed my father?" I asked just above a whisper, gently caressing my pistol.

"Deshana," my grandmother said in a voice pleading for mercy.

"That's what you said, right?" I asked Brianna, ignoring my grandmother.

I could see the fear in Brianna's hazel eyes, but as I studied them closer I saw something like determination swim to the surface as she opened her mouth.

"Devonte wasn't the man I thought he was. Did I love him and plan to spend the rest of my life with him? Yes, but that was before I knew what type of monster he was."

"You mean the type that kills his own father?"

"No, I mean the type that slaughters innocent children."

"Well then, let me be the first to tell you brutality runs in our blood, bitch, and the moment I feel you and your daughter don't deserve to draw another breath, I'll end you both."

"Deshana," my grandmother said again, this time stepping in between me and Brianna.

"Didn't my father banish you from this state? It was your precious Devonte that caused all this shit, anyway!" I yelled in her face, causing other families and future patients to look in our direction.

"Deshana, please. I know you're hurting, sweetheart, but we have to stop all this hate that's destroying our family. He was my son, and I loved him."

"Don't! Because if you loved him, you would've never raised Devonte to hate him. You would've been a better mother from the fucking beginning. So don't ever let me hear you say you loved my father, or I promise those will be your last words," I told her in a fierce whisper.

She opened her mouth to speak, but thought better of it when she saw my grip tightening around my pistol. She may have been my grandmother, my father's mother, but I was my father's daughter, and that meant death could be dealt to anyone.

"Your grandson is dead, which means there's nothing left for you here. I suggest you leave while I still allow you that option."

"Deshana, I—"

"Don't talk to her like that," Brianna said, pushing my grandmother behind her.

"The fuck you say?" I asked, now pulling my gun back out for her to see her fate.

"Listen, this shit has been hard for all of us, and no one wanted it to end this way. When is it gonna be enough? When will you realize that your family is no longer you enemy? We lost two people that were loved tonight, that we didn't have to lose, so how many graves must be dug in the name of revenge?"

"Bitch, listen!"

"Nah, bitch, you listen! Your fucking brother is alive right now, and you're out here ready to kill us? You need to be by his side, because if you ain't learned shit else by now, you should've learned how precious time really is."

I wanted to take my pistol and slap all the teeth and spit out of her mouth, but what she said made sense. Killing either of them in this moment wouldn't give me the satisfaction I wanted, and it wouldn't be what my father would want me to do. He'd tell me *intelligence over emotion*, and he'd be right. He was always right.

As I tucked my gun away, I felt the tears finally come, and I knew it would be awhile before they ever stopped again. I didn't give either woman the pleasure of seeing a single drop fall; instead, I turned away and went in search of the last man on earth I would ever love.

Chapter Three

DJ

It was interesting to watch the movie of my life, as if I hadn't lived it myself and was merely a spectator. I could see my first football game with my dad, the Washington Redskins versus the New York Jets, smell the cheese from the nachos sitting in my lap and hear the crowd of thousands. For a nine-year-old it was the most exciting time of my life, not just because of the game, but because I was doing something very few black boys did: spending quality time with my father.

I'd been a child in years, but with an adult's understanding for a lot of things, because innocence could be replaced no more than time could rewind itself. Still, I was my dad's baby boy, and there wasn't a day that passed when I didn't know it or feel it.

The movie on the screen changed and went back further to when I'd been in second grade and had gotten suspended from school for fighting. Even then I'd known my father and my family weren't people to fuck with, and violence was a utilized tool in life. That's why the ass whooping I got for the fight was so surprising all I could do was cry and plead for understanding.

I thought I hated my dad until he sat my still-tender ass down and explained to me the importance of having an education. I understood somewhat, but the point was driven home when he took me to the streets of Washington D.C. and showed me the people sleeping wherever they could rest their bodies. Conversations with a few made it clear that were it for education, their lives would've been completely different.

Up until that point I understood my father was a powerful man, a man to fear, but in that moment I grasped that he only got that way by being smart. The lesson he said he wanted me to learn was there was a time and place for everything, especially when it came to righting a wrong with violence.

Laying there in my hospital bed, remembering this valuable lesson learned at my father's knee took away the questions I had about what I'd done, because my mother's death had to be answered for. My only regret was my teacher and mentor, my hero, had to be the one to atone for what I'd lost. Some would say I'd lost even more now, but they really don't understand a mother's love and what it does to a person who was forced to grow without it.

I could admit to myself when the searing heat of my brother's bullet hit me, I didn't care if I survived or not. It felt like my whole life had led to that one moment, that one showdown, and if death was to claim me, then let me go while the score was even. Now, laying here listening to the beep and whistle of all the machines keeping me alive, I could only ask myself what would happen next.

Did I win? Was my survival considered a win? And even if my shots had managed to kill Devonte, would I ever stop feeling the hate and anger I could feel pumping through my oxygen-rich blood even in that moment? I had more questions than answers, but prison was a relative certainty, which meant I had time to ask myself these things for years to come. It wasn't something I was looking forward to, but avoidance didn't seem to be an option.

I kept my eyes tightly glued shut as I heard the hospital room door ease open, knowing with every fiber of my being I wasn't ready for police interrogation.

My visitor didn't speak, but I could hear breathing, and a familiar smell was tingling my nose as well as my subconscious. I wasn't exactly sure how long I'd been out or what all had been done to me, but my sense of smell was still working, because that was defiantly gun smoke lingering heavily on whomever was in my presence. Truthfully, I'd rather smell that than the stink of a cop any day.

"I'm so sorry, DJ," I heard her whisper, her voice cracking with evidence of the tears I couldn't see at the moment. My eyes snapped open in surprise at the fact Deshana was standing in my room, and surprise quickly turned to dread at the sight of the pistol she was holding. Deshana was by far my favorite sister just because of all the time we'd spent together, but if there was anyone closer to my father than me, it was her. And that meant my death would now come at her hands.

"Deshana. Wait," I managed to choke out around the tongue that felt like hot asphalt in my mouth. I swallowed as best I could despite the taste of my own blood, needing to explain why I did what I did.

"Don't try to talk. I'm just glad you're alright," she said, coming to my side and standing over me.

She was glad I was alright? Did that mean she forgave me for killing our father, or did she not know the truth? I pointed toward the pitcher of water sitting on the hospital tray table next to my bed, buying time to analyze her motives while organizing my thoughts. I felt like I'd been run over by a train, but I could feel the adrenaline pumping through me as notions of fight or flight threatened to take over my brave space.

"Here you go," she said, handing me a glass of water.

I reached for it clumsily, wasting some of the cool liquid on my blanket and hospital gown on the journey to my mouth.

"How much do you remember?" she asked, sitting in the chair next to my bed.

I was in a private room with just my bed, two chairs, a T.V and a door I assumed was a bathroom, but her presence made the room feel crowded.

"I remember pullin' the trigger," I replied.

"Well, despite everything that happened, he's dead, and I'm happy about that. I just don't understand how dad got caught in the crossfire. I mean, why would he put himself in between you two knowing Devonte would shoot him?"

I wasn't sure who had given her an accounting of the gunplay, but the details were definitely misconstrued. It was time to tread lightly with the facts, because Deshana absolutely had our father's murderous instincts.

"When I got here, Dad was arguing with Devonte, but Brianna was standing in between them. Dad didn't have his gun out, but I could see Tae's clearly, and the look in his eyes changed once he saw me. Dad was trying to reason with him and explain what he'd found out about Keyz, but he wasn't trying to hear it."

"And?" she asked when I stopped talking.

I wasn't sure what she expected me to say, but telling on myself wasn't in my best interest at the moment, so I just shook my head. She finally laid her gun in her lap and buried her face in her hands, the pain escaping from her throat so raw it brought tears to my eyes.

I loved my big sis beyond words and I hated to see her destroyed like this, but what could I do? I'd made the decision to take the life that had given us life and knew I'd have to endure everyone's pain. Maybe one day I'd be man enough to face my own feelings, but in the immediate future there were a million other things to worry about.

"Where are the cops?" I asked, taking another sip of water.

"I don't know. I didn't see any when I got here, but they'll definitely be back."

"I wonder what I'm being charged with?"

"What do you mean?" she asked, wiping tears from her eyes.

Damn, I better start thinking before opening my mouth! Deshana wasn't stupid and if she even thought I killed our father, that was it. It was over. "I mean, didn't you say Tae was dead? How many witnesses do you think they need versus how many they have who saw me shoot the nigga?"

"True, but people have a way of changing their minds or seeing things. Do you really think I'ma let anyone take you away from us after all we just lost?" she asked, giving me the look I'd come to recognize as murder in a bottle.

I knew her loyalty was unshakeable and her determination knew no limits, but this was gonna take more than money.

"How long has it been?"

"They said three hours, but it feels like forever since I got the call."

"Who is *they*, and what call did you get?" I asked, finishing my water and passing her the cup back. I felt weak, yet stronger than I had in longer than I could remember.

"I was referring to your houseguest and your father's mother, both of whom I wanna kill so bad I can fucking taste it!"

"Grandma came down here?"

"She was here before I was, which meant she wasn't far away from the festivities."

We both allowed time for that thought to digest, each of us challenging Devaughn Mitchell and his remedies to fix a situation like this.

"When time permits, we'll definitely clean house," I said.

"Agreed. My question for you is what's the deal with this Brianna chick?"

"What do you mean?"

"I mean I don't understand why she's here still, because her nigga is dead and gone."

"Where is she?"

"The bitch was in the waiting room when I came to find you, but I don't know now."

I touched my forehead gently, remembering the feel of her tears hitting that exact spot as she begged me not to leave the world. I wondered if she felt the same now, knowing I'd killed her man.

"I don't know, but that we can worry about when the time comes. Right now we need to figure out our next move," I replied, trying to readjust myself without screaming out in pain.

"The time has come for that, my nigga, because we don't know what the bitch said, or what she's gonna say to the cops when the time comes. Pops taught us four people can keep a secret if three people are dead."

"Yeah, but that only applies when you don't trust someone."

"I don't trust her!"

"I do."

I could see the argument in her eyes, but she must have seen the unyielding in mine because she didn't push.

"Whatever. The first thing I'ma do is reach out to our people and try to keep the cops away from you so we can get out of town for a while. Then—"

"Nah, don't do that," I said, shaking my head as the plan already began to unfold in my mind.

"Say what?"

"I actually want you to get the cops here A.S.A.P."

"Damn, them some good drugs they put you on, bruh, because you're obviously fucked up! Ain't no self-defense law in VA, which means we need time and space to formulate a plan."

I could see the worry dancing in her eyes, but I knew it was just the shock of the loss that had her brain moving at its current pace.

"Calm down and listen for a second. You're right, there in no self-defense law, but running will make it worse. The reality is Dad wasn't liked by a lot of muthafuckas, but he was respected and feared, and that was the cornerstone of his power. Just because he's gone doesn't mean his power is, and I'm damn sure not giving it up to the vacuum that is these wannabe thugs around here."

"I feel that, but you know we still gotta clean up everything else we got going on. I mean, shit, I still got a naked bitch in my trunk!"

"Ok, first of all, that's reckless, but I get it. And I know everything that has to be done, but you can't do it all, sis. Pops has big shoes to fill, dig me?"

All she could do was nod her head as more tears threatened to spill over onto her cheeks.

"So, what I'ma do is turn myself in, make bail, and go to trial."

"That's it, huh? That's your plan?" she asked with thick sarcasm and irritation.

"This is why Pops sent me to school with the movers and shakers, because he understood in order to be a successful villain, you have to appear the squeaky-clean hero. He put me in a position to cultivate relationships with people bigger than the law and gave me understanding of what really built the world."

"Ok," she said, waiting for the big secret.

"A favor."

"Huh?"

"The world is built on favors. A favor is more valuable than money, not to mention the team of lawyers I've got."

"So you're gonna bet your life on a fucking favor, DJ? I can't talk to you right now, because you're tripping! I'm getting you the fuck outta dodge," she said, pulling her phone out.

"No, what you're gonna do is trust me, because if you can't do that, then get the fuck out."

I hadn't meant to come at her like that, but she was pissing me off because she was only hearing me instead of listening. The look she was giving me said I had her attention, though, because behind all of those tears I could see fight in her, ready to come for me. It was strange watching her bite her tongue. I'd only ever seen her do it with dad until that moment.

"Start over, and break this shit all the way down," she said, climbing in the bed next to me.

Chapter Four

Brianna

My feet moved of their own accord, navigating the hospital hallway with a familiarity I had no idea I possessed since I'd never been here before, but maybe it wasn't the layout. Maybe it was the emotions I couldn't describe pulling me toward him like a puppet on a string. This whole situation was so new and still so emotionally charged that the simplest notions and ideas made no sense, so analyzing our 'connection' at this point was a fool's journey.

"Stay focused," I told myself aloud, taking a deep breath before pushing his hospital room door open. Given the last time I'd seen the handsome brown eyes that were turned on me had been when he'd been lying in his own blood fighting death, I wasn't sure what to expect now.

I stood just inside the door, holding my breath, willing him to move or do anything to indicate how he was feeling inside. It seemed so stupid to ask how he was, but I really wanted to know. I needed to know, and I couldn't explain or put into words what the driving force behind my curiosity was.

"Do you think you love me?" he asked.

His voice was stronger than I'd anticipated, but as sweet to my ears as my daughter's first cries had been.

"I don't know, but I think I want to."

"And why is that?" he asked with the same guarded expression on his face.

I'd heard stories about people looking frail and fragile after surviving the trauma of a gunshot wound, but he looked the exact opposite. In fact, he looked more in control than I'd ever seen him, which made this situation both harder and easier.

Easier because I didn't have to hold his hand or baby him, yet harder because I wanted to hold his hand and baby him.

"What do you want from me, DJ?"

"That's what I'm asking you, Brianna."

"What do you mean?"

"I'm trying to understand why you're still here and why you care. I mean, from what I understand, I just killed the man you loved most in the world. Yet, somehow, here you stand before me looking as if you wanna hold me or something. That ain't normal."

"Is anything about the situation normal?" I asked, thinking about all we'd been through between him kidnapping me, shooting Tae the first time, but then saving our daughter's life when she came premature.

None of this shit was a Lifetime movie, but the truth of the matter was somewhere along the way my heart had opened up to this man. He'd shown himself not to be a man of perfection, but one of change, and that was the hardest man to find.

"You're absolutely right, none of this shit is normal, but now you can have a chance at some type or normalcy for you and Hope."

"What do you mean?"

"I mean you and your daughter are free now. You're free of the violence and everything that comes with it, you're free to just have a good life and enjoy everything you have."

"And what do I have, DJ?"

"Whatever you want. Money ain't an issue, and no one will ever bother either of you again."

"That's your personal guarantee."

"Of course."

"What if I wanted more?"

"Like what?"

"Like maybe for Hope to have a good man in her life and spend time with you. Shit, I can't even get her to sleep!"

At that moment his façade finally cracked a little and he gave me that smile that could infuriate me when my daughter would curl up on his chest and go to sleep. She was still an infant and oblivious to how dangerous DJ was, but for some reason they had a bond I couldn't understand.

"As much as I love little Hope Amazing, I don't think it's a good idea to be around me, for real."

"Why not?"

"Let's not act like you didn't just see me blown my own father's head off, not to mention Tae. My lifestyle just ain't safe for either of you," he said, now avoiding my gaze entirely.

I took another deep breath and prayed my legs would carry me where I wanted to go as I crossed the room to his bedside. I didn't take the chair sitting next to his bed, but instead stood right next to the railing and took his hand in my own. His hands were warm and his fingers strong as they laced with my own, but still he didn't look at me.

"Do you doubt your ability to keep us safe now that all your enemies are dead and the old scores are settled?" I asked, knowing only part of that was true. But knowing this was the only way for us all to survive.

"All my enemies ain't dead," he replied, looking directly at me.

My breath froze in my chest and I prayed my hand wouldn't start sweating in his as I waited for him to elaborate.

"Huh?" I managed to murmur.

"All of my enemies ain't dead. I know how it looks given what I did to my father, but I'm still his son, and if anyone is gonna fill his shoes, it's gonna be me."

"Why can't your sister or someone else do it? What about your dad's wife?"

"I have to do it because I'm Devaughn Mitchell Junior. I have to do it because this is what I was born and raised to do. I know it looks like my father didn't want me in the streets because I was sent away to private school, but he did it that way so I could do more than conquer the streets. He put me in a position to conquer the world if I wanted to! So you see, it has to be me, and I want it to be me."

The passion in his eyes told me just how serious he was and how much he meant what he said, which meant arguing was a waste of my breath. I'd lived with Devontae and been by his side for years when it came to his decision to gangbang and live that life, so I knew what came with that type of power and situation.

But this was different. This nigga was talking like the new Mob was coming, and he was Boss of Bosses. I didn't necessarily wanna buy into that life, but from the outside looking in I'd never know if the truth we'd hidden had come to light or not. And honestly, I wanted to know this man better without the threat of imminent death being the only thing to make my pussy wet.

"Okay, so what's our next move?" I asked.

"Our next move?" he replied, raising a quizzical eyebrow at me.

"You heard me, nigga."

"First of all, I'ma need you to answer my original question."

"Which is?" I asked, even though I already knew where he was going.

"Do you think you love me?"

"Asked and answered. Next question?" I replied, laughing at the mischief swimming in his eyes.

"Okay then. Tell me the story you told everybody else, because for some reason the general consensus is Tae shot my father and me, and I clapped back in self-defense."

"That's basically how I said it went down. I mean, with them two gone, there's no one to challenge us, and I didn't see why you had to go to jail. Hope shouldn't lose you, too."

"Oh, so you did it for Hope, huh?"

I couldn't hide my smile as I finally sat in the chair next to his bed, my hand still firmly in his.

"Don't be an asshole, DJ."

"Okay, alright. What about the witnesses, though?"

"Well, I took a chance on that, hoping you did whatever you did to the cameras like you did last time. As far as the actual people, though, nobody knows what the hell was going on or who started shooting. It helped that Tae was here first, and him and your dad had already been into it, so people saw him with a gun long before you."

"Speaking of which, what happened to the chick he brought in here?"

"Girl? What girl?" I replied confused.

"When we caught up to him out here, we ran down on them at a motel. My sister let her homies light up the parking lot while we went for the room, where we found four of them: two bitches, another dude, and Tae. The dude got hit up, some little, bony black chick is on her way to a fresh hell as we speak, but Tae managed to get over the balcony with some naked redhead."

Just by his description I knew he was talking about Pinky, the Brain, and Ruby, because they were the core of Devontae's team. What I didn't like was that they were all in one fucking room together naked, because I knew Pinky was a ho, and even though I'd never caught them I was pretty sure Ruby had fucked my man. I could only imagine the shit they'd been doing in that room!

"I didn't know nothing about it because I was at your house, but I'll find out if you want me to," I said.

"Yeah, because I don't want no loose ends running around, especially while I'm still in this position."

"Okay. Don't you think we need to get you out of here now? Because the cops are definitely coming back."

"I know they are; in fact, they should be here soon."

"What now?"

"I told Deshana to send for them on her way out after she told you to come see me."

"Okay, I can understand you wanting to see me, but why the fuck would you want the cops? Even with my statement they're gonna arrest you for murder!" I yelled, snatching my hand away from his and jumping out of the chair.

"Calm down and I'll explain," he said patiently, motioning for me to sit back down.

I just crossed my arms and stared at him until he began speaking.

"While the police are here charging me, my legal team will be making bail for me, because they're not gonna put me in jail after what just happened. In the meantime, my sister is reaching out to a few friends who are gonna make this all disappear before it even gets started. All we gotta do is maintain and don't fold. Can you do that?"

I swear he made me wanna hit him in the damn face, because he was trying to downplay a murder charge like it was a traffic ticket. I knew I had to trust he knew what he was doing, though.

"Whatever, where're your car keys?"

"I have no idea, but why?"

"Because I need to go check on Hope. I'm sure she's up screaming her head off by now, wondering where we are."

"She's fine, CJ has her. Plus I need you here."

I couldn't explain the way my stomach suddenly flipped with just that one statement, but I turned away from him and busied myself with a cup of water to hide my expression. Silence filled the room as I drank and thought of what to say that wouldn't sound stupid or girlish.

"Need me here for what?"

"Because you're my star witness, for one."

Of course I was. I don't know why I was trying to read some deep shit.

"And because I heard what you said."

"What do you mean, you heard what I said?" I asked, turning back to face him slowly.

"When I was lying there bleeding, wondering if Heaven had a ghetto and if Jesus was white, I heard you telling me not to die. I felt your tears on my face and your hand in mine," he replied softly.

"I…" I didn't know what to say to that, and any words I had were stuck in my throat by the powerful look he was giving me. Maybe powerful wasn't the right word. There was more of a hunger to it than anything else.

"Come here," he commanded, and before I realized it I was back at his bedside, taking his outstretched hand.

With a gentle tug I was leaning toward him until our lips met in a kiss so tender, but held so many promises of endless possibilities it took my breath away. When his lips parted I drank greedily, taking what he gave and letting him know I could handle the storm that was him.

I know he wanted more for me and Hope, wanted us to know life outside of his violence and crazy world, but he was a risk I needed to take. How often did a person find bad guys who were good? Who were rooted in principle despite life's chaos? I couldn't just walk away.

"Aw, isn't this sweet?" I heard someone say from behind me. It wasn't the comment that broke the spell, it was the sarcasm, and I had some quick shit on my tongue to say as I spun around, but I bit my tongue on that subject.

"Officers, if I'm not mistaken you were asked here, so why are your weapons out?" I asked, standing in front of DJ.

"I'd advise you to shut up, bitch, and move out the way or you're next to die in this hospital."

Chapter Five

Ramona

My breath came in great gasps from my mouth as if I'd been drowning and could just now find the surface. I could feel my heart beating in my chest with the force of a sub-woofer, and even though I expected it to explode any minute, I continued repeating a mantra in my head: *don't panic*. Of course, this was easier said than done when all my mind could see were flames leaping from the barrel pointed in my direction and the sound of thunder rolling reverberating in my ears.

Still, I focused on controlling my breathing, visualizing a different time and place than the cold hospital linoleum I kept seeing myself lying on. And then, like a magician's final trick, it all changed. I couldn't hear the gunshots or smell the stench of bleach and sickness waiting on the air. I couldn't feel the bullet that took me off my feet, nor hear the prayers in my mind for my sweet and innocent baby girl.

Slowly my heart rate began to beat out a regular rhythm, and the smells filling my nostrils were the most pleasant from my childhood of lemons and oranges, with just a hint of sea salt riding the breeze. With these smells came a flood of memories so powerful I could feel the tears siding down my face, but they were tears of joy. Pure, unabashed joy.

Opening my eyes, I saw rows upon rows of lemon and orange trees, their leaves fluttering with the gentle breeze that swayed the thin curtains of my open bedroom window. I could hear waves crashing in the distance and the strong tenor of some long-forgotten singer serenading of a love lost. I could see the sun waving farewell to another day of simple living in these much simpler times, an orange-ish yellow reflecting more beautifully off the water than one could put words to.

These were the memories of my childhood I carried with me and shared with no one, and I closed my eyes again to bask in all their splendor. When I opened my eyes, I fully expected to be in the here and now, but strangely enough I was still looking at the exact same images. How could that be? Unless, was I dead? Was this what Heaven looked like? I couldn't complain about the beauty, but I didn't want to die yet. What would happen to my baby girl? What type of life would she have without me there to love her and guide her and nurture her? I could feel that panic coming on again, but this time I was embracing it instead of fighting it.

My arms felt like overcooked pasta, but still I managed to move them enough to get at the I.V. stuck in my arm. I was expecting all the bells and whistles heard on T.V. once it was removed, but it slipped from my skin without so much as a whisper. It was time to move. That was a clear enough thought in my mind, so why didn't my legs get the memo and do their thing?

After a brief fight with my sheets, I managed to pull myself into a sitting position, but what I saw turned my blood to ice, and for a moment my legs were forgotten. If this was Heaven or some form of afterlife, then it was definitely connected to my past in an unsettling way. The sights and sounds that seemed so familiar weren't just a part of my childhood home. As I gazed around the room done in different pinks and whites, with the pile of assorted stuffed animals at the foot of my bed, and out onto the balcony my father had specially built for me, I felt a chill pass through my body. I wasn't imagining this shit. I was really at home in my bed. Which meant?

"Holy mother of God," I heard a murmur from a figure sitting in the wicker chair right next to my bed.

My head immediately snapped in that direction, but what I saw was impossible to explain. It was me. Not me at that moment, but me as I'd been as a teenager. The curly black hair, the fresh sun-kissed skin, the huge black eyes framed by those long, silky lashes all the girls would come to envy, and that body not even an oil barrel my favorite olives came in could hide. I was looking at me so many years ago, but it wasn't me. Something in those eyes, those endlessly black eyes, told me I wasn't seeing the younger version of myself.

"Who are you?" I asked, and the gravel in my voice was a shock to both of our ears. Why the fuck did I sound so man-ish?

"M-m-mama?" she replied, her disbelief as evident as my own.

There was no way I heard her right, and proof of that was in the insistent buzzing taking up space in my brain. Something was wrong, terribly wrong, but I had no time for further analysis before I was flat on my back, looking up at the canopy covering my bed. And then I heard nothing.

Then I was dreaming, but it was a great dream because I was in his arms again, and we were making love. Time stood still as he listened to my body and whispered loving replies back, pushing me to new heights only to catch me when I fell. I could see his infectious smile and feel its warmth all over me, taste the raw passion in every kiss he gave. I could feel those strong hands bring out every girlish impulse I tried to hide as he pulled me close and wrapped me in his embrace. But too soon I felt him slipping away from me, felt his fingers slip right through my own, and I was thrust back into that world of unspeakable pain I'd lived in from the moment I awoke without him.

I opened my eyes again, expecting to see the house we used to share, but instead I was once again in my childhood bedroom looking up at the only other man who'd ever had my heart the way my husband did.

"Papa? Papa, why are you crying?" I asked, wishing I could wipe his tears away.

"A miracle! You've come back to us, my dear, and it is nothing short of miracle!" he exclaimed, showering my face with kisses.

While I understood I would forever be his baby girl, I did think all this was a bit excessive.

"I had the weirdest dream, Papa. Actually, it seemed like a lot of dreams," I said, trying to sit up.

"No, no, lay still until the doctor comes to examine you," he replied, pushing me back down gently.

"Examine me? For what?"

"Sweetheart, do you know where you are?"

"Of course I do, I'm in Sicily. I don't know how I got here or why I'm here instead of my own house, but I could never forget my childhood summers."

"Good, good," he said, smiling.

"Papa, are you okay?"

"I've never been better in my life, but just humor me for a moment. Where is your house?"

"Seriously? My main house is in VA, which is in the U.S. of A, in case you were wondering," I replied, wondering if this was Alzheimer's setting in already on him.

"Okay, tell me, what is the last thing you remember?"

"I…"

This question did cause me just a little more difficulty because for some reason it seemed like my memories were out of order. The biggest one seemed to be Devaughn, so it made sense to start there and work forward.

I'd known dating him was wrong since he was one of my parolees, but there was just something about him that drew me to him. I had to find out what it was, but muthafuckas kept trying to kill him! I got shot and he saved my life, then he got shot and I saved him from prison again. Then there was the war. It seemed like he was fighting everyone, from rival blood sets to his own leaders of his blood set, but he was determined to survive. Not just survive, but to live.

Then there was Keyz. Thinking about that scandalous whore put a taste of bile in my throat, making me wanna vomit until my head popped off. I had to stay focused, though. She shot Devaughn, but he didn't die, and me and Candy took care of him in secret. Candy, she had DJ. Wait, they were both pregnant, and the other one's name was D-D-Devontae! Okay, so we brought the war to Keyz, and she returned the favor.

Deshana came home to help, but Jordyn betrayed us all. I got shot again, but so did Keyz. Devaughn came back to me, but I had to end it while there was still a chance, so I went after Keyz at the hospital and...

"She shot me! She killed my baby!" I exclaimed in fury, feeling that panic rising again with a swiftness.

"Shh, calm down, calm down," my father said, taking my hand.

How did he expect me to calm down when the last thing I remembered was bleeding out on a hospital floor and praying I didn't lose the miracle Devaughn and I had created!

"Dad, you don't understand. She killed—"

"Mama?" she whispered.

Her voice cut through all the fog and screaming in my brain, and I was finally able to see her standing at the foot of my bed. I thought I'd imagined her before because she looked so much like me, but now, looking at her closer, I could see her father in every breath she took. Those eyes may have been the same beautiful onyx as my own, but the intelligent, almost eerie calculation behind them only came from one man.

"It can't be," I whispered, rubbing my stomach.

She was no more than a few months old inside of me when I was shot, so there was no way this girl standing in front of me could be my daughter.

"Dad, who is she?"

"I'd like you to meet Isabella Petras Mitchell. Your daughter."

"Impossible."

"And yet you know it's entirely possible, because as you said yourself so long ago, she's a miracle."

"But. B-but, how long? How old? What happened?" I stammered, trying to make sense of what made absolutely no sense.

"As the Americans say, it is a long story, but I will do my best if you just bear with me. You were shot in the throat on the same night your husband came out of his coma, and as fate would have it, you were thrust into a coma of your own. Miraculously, Isabella survived safely in your womb. I brought you home to Italy, and when the time came you delivered a healthy 6 pound, 3 ounce baby girl."

"But how?"

"The wonders of modern day medicine surpass my limited knowledge of the world, my child. All I concerned myself with was taking care of both of you in hopes you would one day come back to us."

"How-how long?" I finally managed to ask, knowing I shouldn't try to overload myself with information, but needing answers.

At this question he looked from me to my daughter and back to me. Aside from saying *mama*, she had yet to utter a word. She merely stood there as waves of tears cascaded down her young face. I could imagine how shocking all this must be for her.

"Bella will be thirteen years old this year," my father replied softly.

"Thirteen. Thirteen years? I've been unconscious for thirteen years?"

I wasn't sure how one even began to wrap their mind around some shit like that! Every day of those five years with Devaughn had been agonizing because I never knew what day would be the last, either way. I just knew I couldn't give up hope.

"So I've been here, in this bed, for thirteen years?"

"You have."

"Okay, so it's safe to say I missed a lot."

This comment earned me the most beautiful and endearing smile from my daughter as she moved to the other side of the bed to take my hand.

"And I'm assuming the bullet I took to the throat is why I sound like an eighty-year-old smoker now?"

"Your voice is a thing of beauty, Ramona. I could listen to you talk for the rest of my life," he replied with a huge grin on his face.

"Well, you're my father, so you have to put up with it. Let's see what my husband thinks. Where's Devaughn?"

My question was met with a silence I didn't like, and now the tears flowing from my daughter's eyes didn't seem to be the ones of happiness from a moment ago.

Growing up with the education I did in both the street life and what society deemed acceptable, I'd learned just how cruel fate could be. Yet my faith in love wouldn't allow me to believe that once again my soulmate and I had somehow passed each other like flights over the Atlantic. No one deserved that cruelty.

"Papa, I asked you a question. Where is my husband?"

Aryanna

Chapter Six

Devontae

It wasn't the sound of voices raised in anger that woke me up, but what was it? Lying there, I tried to take stock of my surroundings, but the only thing I knew for certain was I had absolutely no idea where I was. This probably should've surprised me, and it did, but not as much as waking up at all did.

I didn't have to be a doctor to know how bad a gunshot wound was, and considering the visions I'd had of my long-dead mother, I knew death had been upon me as I bled out on the hospital floor. She'd told me she'd protect me, though, and it would seem she had kept her word to me. Which meant I had to keep mine to her, but first I needed to know what the fuck was going on and why everyone was screaming.

"Tae," she whispered, tugging on my arm again, helping me identify what had brought me back to the land of the living.

"Where are we, Pinky?" I asked, taking her hand in my own, glad she was alive and by my side.

"I don't know, but wherever we are, we damn sure ain't wanted here."

"What do you mean?"

"That's what all that arguing is about in there: the fact we're here. Whoever owns this house wants us anywhere but under this roof, and they want you dead."

With this statement I felt the adrenaline coursing through my veins. Me dying wasn't an option, not until I fulfilled the promise I'd made to my mother, but I was in no way prepared to defend myself, which only left me with one option. It was time to run.

The shadows were heavy in the room, but I could still see dawn's light fighting its way through the blinds over the window. From the looks of it, we were in a spare bedroom, both of us flat on our backs on the only bed available. The only other furnishing was a cheap dresser that sat directly under the window, but it would aid in our escape.

"Can you move?" I asked her, taking a mental inventory of my own mangled body.

"Yeah, but it hurts like hell. It hurts just to breath."

"Same here. We gotta get out of here, though, because we're in no condition to fight."

"We don't even know where we are, Tae. It's the dude who wants you dead."

"Huh?"

"The argument is between two females and one dude. I could only make out bits and pieces, but the women are on your side and just wanna keep you safe."

"Who are they?" I asked, wondering who in the world would be advocating for me.

"I don't know, but they keep saying they want your side of the story before any decisions are made."

Allowing that thought to roll around in my brain a little, I continued studying my surroundings in hopes of maybe finding some type of weapon. Pinky and I had on hospital gowns, which meant we were literally asshole naked and in need of an equalizer, quick!

The bedroom door was to my left and Pinky was on my right, which helped in the aspect of me protecting her. The major problem was I couldn't feel my left arm, but I could see it was in a sling strapped down to my chest. Analyzing all this brought me back to one thought that continued to echo loud and clear in my mind: run!

"Okay, Pinky, listen."

"Please stop calling me that. Josh is – he's dead, and without him I'm just Amber."

There were no words for me to give her because I understood exactly how she felt. We'd both lost someone we loved very much, and no amount of time could heal that wound. The best we could do was live so they hadn't died in vain.

And murder everyone who had contributed to their deaths in any way.

I laced my fingers with hers to show her I was with her. "Amber I don't know who's arguing, but they're not deciding our fate. We are. I need you to look out that window and tell me what you see."

"Okay."

I could feel her trying to build up the energy it would take for her to move, and I gave her hand another reassuring squeeze before letting it go.

Slowly she managed to sit up without screaming bloody murder, but at the rate she was breathing I knew she wanted to. One baby step at a time, she shuffled until she could lean her weight against the dresser and part the blinds.

"Are we on the ground floor?" I asked, hopeful.

"No."

"Shit!"

"It gets worse."

"What is it?"

"All I see is trees."

"What do you mean?"

"I mean, wherever we are, this house is backed up against the woods, and we're definitely in the sticks."

Talk about a fish out of water! The only time we saw trees and shit in New York was when we traveled up state or if we went to central park. This could be good, though, if we used it to our advantage.

"How far of a drop is it?" I asked.

"At least two stories. Do you hear that?"

Instead of responding I gave all my attention to listening to whatever had caught hers, but all I heard was us breathing.

"I don't hear shit," I whispered.

"Exactly."

At first I didn't understand what she meant, but then it registered that there was an absence of voices.

"Tae."

Her thought was interrupted by the sound of feet on wooden stairs, and it was definitely more than one person. My body screamed in protest as I scrambled into a sitting position, and when I finally stood up I was looking at more stars swimming through my vision than they had on the flag. Still, I pushed on and moved around the room until I was standing directly in front of Amber.

I didn't have a damn clue on how I could stop anyone, but I was down to show them Keyz's son wasn't no bitch. The knob turned slowly, the door opened, and in walked my grandma followed by the nurse from the hospital and some nigga I didn't know.

"What are you doing out of bed, baby? And where's Amber?" my grandma asked.

The relief I felt almost made me pass out right there, but instead I took the shoulder of support she offered and sat back on the bed. Amber followed my lead, sitting on the bed beside me.

"Where are we, and who's he?" I asked, nodding toward the brown-skin nigga with dreads and a scowl on his face still posted in the doorway.

"Don't worry about who I am, just know that you in my house," he replied hostilely.

"Maurice, chill!" Tiffany said, putting a hand on his chest.

"I'm chillin'. Y'all better holla at him."

I didn't know who the dude was or what his issue was with me, but he did look vaguely familiar, in a way I couldn't put my finger on.

"You're safe, baby, and that's all that matters."

"You sure about that?" I asked, still staring the dude down in case he wanted to make a move.

"I heard you all arguing, and I know he wants Tae dead," Amber chimed in.

"I don't want the little nigga dead, I just don't want him in my muthafuckin' house."

"Maurice."

"Nah, young, he killed my muthafuckin' brother, Joe. And now you want me to help hide him out? Where they do that at?"

"Ayo, my man, I don't know nobody named Joe, but if he got killed, then either he was gunning for me or on the wrong side of this war," I said, not liking his tone in the slightest.

"You trying to be funny, slim?" he asked, stepping into the room.

"A'ight, both of you chill the fuck out and don't say nothing else to each other! Maurice, I mean it!" Tiffany said, putting a hand on his chest.

This nigga had to be 50+ years old, so even shot up like I was, giving him an ass whooping would be child's play. I owed Tiffany, though, so I'd bit my tongue until he opened his mouth again.

"Devontae, tell me what happened once you got to the hospital," my grandma said.

"Once Tiffany told me I couldn't see Pinky, I mean Amber, until tomorrow, I was leaving when I saw Brianna coming down the hall. Devaughn was with her, so I pulled my pistol and tried to get a clear shot, but she jumped in between us, talking some shit about my mother and him not being related. She said he'd just found out, and that meant I was as much his son as DJ, so we had to end it."

"And then?"

"Before I could agree or disagree, DJ came down the hall shooting, so Brianna and Devaughn got in between me and him. They tried explaining the same shit to him, but he wasn't hearing it because all he wants is revenge for his mother. Devaughn – Dad – couldn't see the look in DJ's eyes, but I could, and I knew what was gonna happen. I shot him, but I was too late because he's already pulled the trigger."

"Back up, who shot Devaughn?" Tiffany asked.

"What do you mean, *who shot Devaughn*? DJ shot him."

The looks I got from that statement gave me a feeling of unease, because it seemed like the first time anybody had heard that part of the story.

"Grandma?"

"Continue, baby," she said, looking at Tiffany.

"Well, I shot him, and I hope you're getting ready to tell me him and Brianna are both dead."

"Why Brianna? I thought you loved her?"

"I did. I do, but something happened when she was with DJ. When I saw her, she wasn't acting like she'd been kidnapped."

"You see, Ms. Gladys, I knew I wasn't trippin'! When I got to where the shooting was, she was huddled over DJ's body crying and shit, and that's why when she told me who she was I started to call her ass out on it," Tiffany said.

"So she's alive?" I asked, not sure how I felt about that right now.

"She is, and so is DJ," my grandmother said.

I knew exactly how I felt about that revelation, and the look of undisguised hatred on Amber's face mirrored only a piece of what I felt. The look I gave her said it all: he was only alive for the moment.

"So, you didn't shoot Devaughn?" he asked from the doorway.

"Yo, who are you?" I asked again.

"I'm Maurice, Tiffany's husband and your uncle."

Now shit started to make sense, and I could understand why he'd been as hostile as he had.

"Why did you think I shot my dad?"

"Because that's what Brianna said," my grandmother replied softly.

If she would have pulled a gun on me at that exact moment, I couldn't have been any more surprised. To know the woman I'd loved and cherished for more than half of my life had betrayed me this way left me utterly speechless. I couldn't believe it, but as I looked into everyone's eyes, I saw the truth that couldn't be hidden.

"But why? Why would she say that?" I murmured.

"I don't know, baby, and we may never know the answer to that question. What I do know is it doesn't matter at this point. All that matters is getting you better and keeping you safe."

"How can you say it doesn't matter? The police will be coming for him," Amber said, taking my hand.

"No, they won't because they think he's dead," Tiffany replied.

"Whose idea was that?" I asked.

"Believe it or not, it was Brianna's," my grandmother said.

This surprised me because it was in complete contrast to what I was learning about my baby's mother, but then again, maybe thinking of me as dead and gone appealed to her conscience.

"She said the only way DJ would stop hunting you was if he believed you were dead, and I agreed with her. I know my son, and he would've raised DJ to keep pushing until there was nothing left."

"So that's it? You expect me to tuck my tail between my legs, run away, and let them raise my daughter like one big, happy fucking family?" I raged.

"Nah, young, that's not what you do. You lick your wounds, heal up, and learn when to say that one word no nigga wants to hear in this game," Maurice said patiently.

I looked to him expectantly, and this made him smile.

"Checkmate."

Chapter Seven

Deshana

The walk from the hospital back to my car was one of the longest of my life, and at times I didn't know if I'd make it.

"What's wrong? Baby, what happened?" JuJu asked once I was back behind the wheel, but the words wouldn't come. Finally, I just dissolved into a puddle of tears and was grateful my wife could simply hold me in this moment of devastation.

I'd held it together while in front of DJ because not even he could understand what it was like to live this nightmare for the second time in one lifetime. The pain was worse than I could remember, maybe because I knew it was certain this time. There would be no miraculous recoveries. My daddy was really and truly gone. So what now? Who was I if not Devaughn Mitchell's daughter?

"He's—he's gone, Ju."

"Who, baby?"

"My daddy. My daddy is dead," I sobbed in her arms, wishing the world would just go back and take us all with it to whatever hell awaited.

For a while we stayed like that, my wife holding me as she'd done whenever I'd needed her. She was the only person outside of my father I could be completely vulnerable with and bare my soul to, and as painful as it would be, I knew she'd help me put my world back together

"Tell me," she said, softly stroking my head and holding me tighter.

I told her what happened from the moment I walked into the hospital until I'd lost it in her arms, feeling the guilt weigh me down even more because I knew it was my fault. That was something I had to carry with me forever. I deserved nothing less because I'd known better.

Parents may do thing to piss their children off or cause them discomfort in the moment, but they're rarely, if ever, wrong. My father's wisdom had saved his life more than once, and I should've trusted that.

"Who am I without him, Ju? Besides you, he was everything in this world to me, and now he's just gone. Who am I?" I asked, searching her eyes for the answer to a question I would forever ask myself.

Cupping my face in her hands, she pressed her lips gently to mine before kissing the paths of my tears. And in that same motion, she cocked back and slapped me hard enough to put the taste of blood in my mouth.

"Who are you? You're Deshana Mitchell! You're a gangster, a killer, my wife, but more importantly, you're always and forever the daughter of the legendary Devaughn Mitchell. Don't ever ask me that question again, understand?"

My shock at being hit gave way to raw, consuming anger, but it wasn't directed at JuJu, because I knew she was right. It was disrespectful of me to question who I was like my father's lessons had been for naught, and I wouldn't tarnish his memory that way.

"You're right," I replied, swallowing the blood in my mouth. "So, what's the plan?"

My response to this was to pull out my cell phone and call the law offices of Merril Lynch, where I retained counsel for DJ. Then I called and anonymously let the detectives working the case know DJ was awake and preparing to run.

"Do you know what you're doing?" she asked.

"It's DJ's plan. He said the quickest way to get the cops to him and get shit moving was to act like he was avoiding them."

"Until he gets bail?"

"Yeah, we took care of that before I left his room. According to him, if this is played right, then he'll be back at the house in a couple hours, and he's calling a family meeting."

"Sounds like your brother is stepping up quickly."

Her comment mirrored my thoughts exactly, but it was necessary because like he'd said, our father had big shoes to fill. Out of the corner of my eye I saw my grandmother leaving the hospital and climbing behind the wheel of a black BMW parked next to DJ's Bugatti. I knew she felt my stare of hatred, but she was smart enough not to even look in my general direction. Still, her time would come.

"Are we going to your brother's house?" JuJu asked, breaking the spell I was under.

"Yeah, I want you to follow me in my dad's car. We need to deal with this bitch in the trunk and get ready to head to NY so we can finish up the takeover."

"Baby, the homies up there can handle that, right now we should be here with the family," she replied, taking my hand in hers.

"Nah, I owe it to my pops to see it through to his conclusion. That's what he would've wanted."

Nodding her head, she gave me a quick kiss before getting out and gong to my dad's car. It had been a birthday present from me, and I'd never get rid of it, but it was too soon for me to be behind the wheel.

Once JuJu was in the car, I led the way back to the main house, not sure how I was gonna tell Belinda her husband was gone. And what about Isabella? She'd lost two parents to tragedy and violence at the age when she needed both the most. Hopefully her grandfather would want us all together. Who was gonna tell Sharday? Even as the question ran through my mind, I knew it had to be me and no one else.

She'd done her best to ignore who our father was, but deep down she knew like the rest of us his death wouldn't come in a peaceful slumber. Guys like him went out the same way they lived, but I don't think even he could've seen one of his own children taking his life. Yet he let it happen, because right or wrong, he'd never willingly harm one of his own. He wasn't made like that.

Coming up the driveway, I could see people standing out front of the main house, which meant avoidance even for the moment wasn't an option.

"Take my car down to DJ's house," I told JuJu, giving her a knowing look.

"Why is she driving Devaughn's car?" Belinda asked, her tone trying to downplay the fear I could see in her eyes.

CJ hadn't said a word. She just stood there holding a little hope, but I could feel all she wanted to say.

"Why is she driving his car, Deshana? What happened?" she asked again, near hysteria.

I couldn't find the words. I opened my mouth to try to speak, but I couldn't find the words I knew would shatter her world. I'd seen my father with women before, and I'd heard of the love he and my mother shared once upon a time, but not since Ramona had I witnessed him give himself completely to anyone the way he had Belinda.

If there were no words to describe their love, then there could be none to describe the loss of it now. Saying *I'm sorry* just didn't seem like enough.

"Belinda, he loved you, and you know that."

"Oh God, oh God, please don't say it. Deshana, please!" she begged me, sinking to her knees as if crashed by the weight of the world.

I didn't say it, but I didn't have to.

"Belinda."

But I was talking to her back because she was running back into the house, her wails causing baby Hope to weep for the grandfather she'd never know.

"Is–is DJ?" CJ finally found the courage to whisper in my direction.

"No. He was shot twice, but he survived. He'll be home soon, and he's gonna need you. Are you up to it?"

Her response was nodding her head, because I don't think she trusted her own voice in that moment. Tears of relief seemed like they wanted to choke her as she rocked and soothed Hope, and I wondered if DJ knew she was more than a little in love with him.

If he was truly his father's son, then he was oblivious, but I'd do my part to open his eyes, because she had to be better fit than that bitch Brianna.

"I've got some business to handle down at the house, so I want you and the baby to stay up here for a while. See if you can help calm Belinda down."

"Okay," she replied without hesitation.

Pulling my phone out, I dialed Sharday's number as I walked toward DJ's house, but it was a man who answered instead of my big sister.

"Who is this?"

"This Ready, who dis?" came the reply.

Ready Roc was one of the li'l homies, but he was an up-and-coming rapper, so it only made sense to have him around DayDay so he could learn the game and protect her. His skills on the mic were only matched by his pistol play.

"Ready, it's twin, what's crackin'?"

"What's crackin', big homie? We in Memphis doing a show right now. DayDay on stage killin' it!"

I could hear the crowd in the background, and it made me smile because no matter what had happened, Sharday hadn't wasted her talent. I know that always made our pops proud. I hated to cut her tour short, but we needed her home now more than ever.

"How long are you supposed to be in Tennessee?" I asked.

"I think it's two more shows, and then we go to Georgia."

"Change of plans, I need you to bring her home."

"Oh yeah? You know she's not gonna like that."

"Yeah, I know, but it's serious."

"Say no more, I'll have the bus headed that way within the hour. What you want me to tell her, though?"

That was one helluva question, because she was automatically gonna know something was wrong, but this wasn't news I could break over the phone.

"Just tell her we need her home," I said, opening the door to DJ's house and following my sense of smell to the living room.

"I gotchu, homie."

"And Ready, don't let her out of your sight."

"I won't," he replied, disconnecting the call.

Putting my phone back in my pocket, I took my jacket off and laid it across the back of the couch, looking at the feast laid before me on the living room floor.

"Good idea, putting plastic down," I said.

"I'm not new to this, babe," she replied, winking and rolling up her sleeves.

"Damn, bitch, you stink! You smell like three different types of cum and sweat. No wonder you wasn't ready when we came for you."

The gag in her mouth made her replies muffled, but my purpose for removing it was so I could get to those pearly white teeth.

"Fuck you, bitch!" she spat, hate making her eyes blaze as she struggled uselessly against her zip ties.

"You could never get that pussy, sweetheart, because it belongs to me," JuJu said, giving me a wink as she unrolled the tools I'd need for this job.

Ordinarily I liked to take my time when I worked, but DJ would be home soon, and I couldn't leave his house a mess.

"Baby, you got my cigar?" I asked JuJu.

"Right here," she replied, lighting the Cuban and passing it to me after a few puffs.

"Now, first things first. I notice that little brand you have on your arm there, and you're too young for that to have been mandatory, which means you must be important to the Blood movement. I'm not gonna ask you who you are because that's too easy. No, I want you to beg to tell me. Seeing as how me and my beautiful wife here are respectfully Crippin', I'm gonna have to cover up your 'dog paw' because it offends us."

Before she could protest I took my cigar and added a fourth circular burn to the three she already had on her right arm. Three burns was a badge of honor, the almighty dog paws symbolizing Blood, but four meant they were no longer part of the nation. They were food.

She took the burn with only a sharp intake of breath, but she didn't scream, and I liked that. Now my goal was clear.

"You know, JuJu, we could start with her nipples since she's naked. What do you think?"

"Whatever you want, babe."

"Hmm. Give me the pliers and clamp her mouth open."

It'd been my experience that pulling teeth would break the toughest muthafuckas, but this wasn't about that. I simply wanted to do something that would make me feel better and make my daddy smile, wherever he was.

"You may feel a little pressure," I warned as I clamped down on one of her back molars with the needle-nose pliers.

Slowly I twisted until her screams filled the air along with my laughter, and when they were at their peak, I snapped part of the tooth off.

"Oops, gotta go back and get the rest." By the time I dug the tooth fragments out of her gums, the aroma of fresh piss was added to the mixture of smells coming from her. And by the time I'd removed two more teeth, I could tell she wanted to tell me every secret she'd ever had or heard in her life.

"Baby, I'm being impolite. Would you like a chance to play with her?" I asked JuJu, who had thus far been observing with a smile.

"You know I would."

I passed her the pliers and sat back on the couch to observe my wife work. I never tired of this bond we shared, because in truth I know something within me was fucked up for enjoying these little sessions. Despite that, though, JuJu loved me unconditionally and didn't just accept this part of me, she understood and identified with it in her own way. We really were two halves of the same whole.

"Mmm, baby, you're making my pussy wet," I told her, loving the screams she had coming from that bitch's mouth as she savagely yanked another tooth.

"I know what does it for you, sweetheart. Should we take it to the next level?"

"What did you have in mind?"

Her response was to simply hold up the one tool we never left home without: a razor.

"I do wanna know what's inside this nasty bitch that got her smelling like this," I said, moving back to the floor to join them.

At the sight of the razor her screams took on a different pitch, a more urgent sound than just the *please don't mutilate me!*

"Ten words or less," I told her when I released the clamp prying her mouth open.

"I'm-I'm pregnant, please!" she sobbed, coughing up blood and tooth fragments.

"You're lying," I replied dispassionately.

"Test me, I'm pregnant!"

All I could do was look at JuJu to see how she felt about this latest revelation. I knew what we were both capable of, so it was all a question of what we were willing to live with.

"Ju?" I asked.

"It's your call."

What was unspoken in that moment was our own wants for a child and the struggle that had come with it. So, could we now kill one?

"Who's the father?" I asked.

The answer was in the fear in her eyes and the tears that wouldn't cease, no matter how much she sniffled.

"Oh, hell nah."

"Help! Somebody help!" CJ came in the house screaming. The first thing I noticed was she was covered in blood. But the more alarming thing was Hope was nowhere in sight.

"What is it? Where's the baby?" I demanded.

"At the — at the house, but it's – it's—"

"Spit it out, goddammit!" I yelled.

"Belinda killed herself!"

Aryanna

Chapter Eight

DJ

"Bri, slowly step aside and don't say anything else," I told her, already wishing I could pump a bullet in those cops' faces for the way they talked to her.

I understood they thought they had arrived just in time to stop a murderer from escaping, but that was no reason to be rude. Once Bri moved, I saw the voices belonged to two fat white guys who obviously had to shoot their suspects, because a foot chase just wasn't gonna happen.

One stood about 5'10" with thin wisps of what used to be blonde hair attempting to cover his baldness, while his partner was half a foot shorter and had enough dignity to give up the fight with his hair, so his dome was squeaky clean. The only things identical about the two were the Glock 40s they were holding tightly and the *shoot-first* look in their eyes.

"Gentlemen, how can I help you?" I asked pleasantly.

"We'll ask the questions, smartass," the taller one replied, circling around my bed so they positioned themselves on both sides of me.

"Just remember that black lives matter, and I'm definitely unarmed."

Only one of these statements was true since I'd convinced Deshana to leave me her pistol, but if they had to find out the truth, then it was too late for us all.

"Devaughn Mitchell Junior, you are under arrest for the murder of Devontae Briggs. You have the right to remain silent. Anything you say can and will be held against you in the court of law. You have the right to an attorney. If you cannot afford an attorney, then one will be provided to you by the courts. Do you understand these rights as I've read them to you?" the shorter cop concluded.

"Indeed I do, sir."

"You got him, Tony?" the taller one asked.

"Yeah, Paul, cuff him."

Holstering his gun, Paul did just that with absolutely no resistance from me. Even though it was only my right arm being handcuffed to my bed, I still didn't like the restricted movement, and I actually questioned whether I'd made the right decision.

"Okay. I'm Detective Tony Miller, and that's my partner Detective Paul Davis. Would you like to tell us what happened here in the early morning hours?"

So this must be what good cop, bad cop looks like. One comes in overly hostile and then the other tries to placate and act like we maybe could be friends if I'd just tell on myself. How in the hell did cop shows ever last on T.V.?

"I have nothing to say until my attorney is present."

"Is she your attorney?"

"No."

"Then she can get the fuck out while we talk," Detective Davis ordered.

"I ain't going nowhere," Brianna replied, sitting back in the chair next to my bed.

I saw the look the cops exchanged as Detective Miller moved toward Bri, and suddenly I could smell death in the air again. "Don't touch her," I warned in a polite whisper. I could feel the cold steel of the gun beneath my left leg, reassuring me control of this situation was still mine if I wanted it.

My warning to the cop only caused a slight hitch in his giddy-up, but my hospital room door opened before things could get real like an old western.

"Ah, detectives, so glad you could make it. I'm Ms. Lynch, attorney for Mr. Mitchell, and here are his bond papers," she said, handing them a folder of documents accompanied with a sexy smile.

Victoria Lynch was not what was expected in a lawyer, or a woman, for that matter. She stood 5'6 and weighed every bit of 210 pounds easy, with lightly bronzed skin one might call copper. She wore her hair in a bob perfected only by Ms. Patti LaBelle and she had a smile that could transform any room into one where she was the center of attention.

She was beautiful, intelligent, confident, and more than capable, but if someone made the mistake of thinking she'd be weak or insecure because of her size, then they had the game fucked up. When we'd met at a mutual friend's house a couple years ago, she looked me dead in the eyes and proclaimed she was big and sexy, and asked if I could handle it.

We'd fucked some furniture up answering that question. She was only 23, but she was a woman in every sense of the word, and that only added to her skills as a lawyer. That was evidenced by how fast she'd secured my bond on a murder charge.

"Is this legit, Tony?" Detective Davis asked.

"Looks that way, Paul. He's on a one million dollar bail, take the cuffs off." His dissatisfaction was evident in all the shit he was mumbling under his breath, but it didn't matter so long as he turned my black ass loose.

"See you soon," he said before they left the room. I made sure to wave so there were no hard feelings.

"Thanks, Victoria," I said.

"No problem, handsome. How are you holding up?"

"I'm alive, so I guess that counts."

"You damn right it does, and I appreciate if you stay that way. Now, tell me what went down so I know what we're up against."

I proceeded to run it all down to her with Brianna's help, getting as close to the truth as I dared without compromising her position. When we were done, she spent several minutes in contemplative thought before turning that gorgeous smile my way.

"Well, given how sticky this situation is, I think the D.A. will listen to reason, but if he won't, I'll just sic my daddy on him."

I laughed at this because I knew her father was no joke, and he kept my father out of shit many times before.

"Okay. I need another favor from you, though."

"And what's that, but be mindful I'm engaged now, DJ," she replied with a devilish grin.

I had to swallow my smile because Brianna was giving me a look I'd never seen from her before, and it carried some heat with it, too.

"I'll clarify. I need a favor from Victoria and not Tory, okay?"

"That's better. Now, what can I do for you?"

"I want you to handle my father's will and estate. I'm not sure how massive it is, but I know the old man cleaned up a lot of his money in the last decade."

"That's no problem, I'm sure my father should have some idea since he's handled a lot of your father's affairs. It's still surreal to me. I mean, I never thought your dad would die. I know that sounds stupid and childish."

"Actually, I know exactly what you mean," I told her, feeling that gnawing begin in my stomach again.

"When will you have the service?" she asked.

"I don't know, not for a week at least so I can get my little sister back from Italy."

"Do you think you're gonna have to fight her family over there for her?"

This was a question and problem I hadn't even considered. Isabella's grandfather was old school Sicilian, which meant another was going up against him, and I didn't even wanna entertain that notion right now.

"I don't know. I'll let my sisters deal with that," I replied.

"Smart choice, because you're a hot head." Now it was my turn to smile at her. "Alright, is there anything else I can do for you, handsome?"

I could feel Bri staring at me again, so I chose to have a little fun.

"Nah, I'm good, beautiful. But I appreciate you, and I appreciate the way you're wearing that pantsuit."

"Black Billionaire, baby," she replied, laughing and waving as she disappeared out the door.

"Really, DJ?" Brianna said, clearly irritated.

I couldn't hold my laughter in anymore, and this earned me a look of complete hostility.

"You're such an asshole!" she huffed, crossing her arms.

"I'm sorry, I'm just fucking with you. Come on, let's get out of this damn hospital," I said, pulling the covers back and putting the .45 back on safety.

"You were gonna shoot them?" she asked, wide-eyed.

"I'd warned them first, so it was on them what the next move would be."

"You're crazy," she said, shaking her head, but she couldn't hide her smile. "I couldn't save your shirt, but I managed to keep your sweats and boxers."

"Where are they?"

"Hold on, I'll be right back."

While she was gone I made the mile-long trip to the bathroom, thinking the whole time I'd pass out from the pain in my chest. Fuck what I thought I knew, getting shot hurt! I guess this was better than the alternative of not feeling pain at all. The way I was feeling actually made me think of my pops, because he's been shot several times before and had survived. That took a special kind of muthafucka.

"DJ, where are you?" she called out.

Shuffling back out into the room I found Bri waiting with a new nightgown to go over my sweats and some paper slippers for my feet.

"What happened to my shoes?"

"To much blood on them to save them. Get dressed, I'll be in the hall."

"Wait, you ain't gonna help me?"

"Nope. Want me to call Tory back?" she asked with a sarcastic smile on her face.

"Touché."

"Oh, and by the way," she said, lifting the gown to reveal two pistols laying side-by-side.

I recognized one immediately because it was mine, which meant the other had to be Devonte's.

"I was wondering when this part of the story would be explained."

"It's simple, amidst all the chaos the guns were forgotten, and so I hid them. When the cops came the first time, I played dumb, again counting on you not leaving video footage, and I prayed no one else saw me."

"Who are you?" I asked, half-jokingly.

"Just a woman who wants the same thing you do."

"And what is it you think I want?"

"Peace."

I chose not to correct that notion, but I think we both understood peace was a novel idea that involved a happy ending. Seeking that was like chasing the Holy Grail.

"I'm ready when you are," I said, giving a tug on my hospital gown and watching her expression as it came off, revealing my nakedness. She looked me over from head to toe and didn't blush once before meeting my eyes again.

"Nice dick, but you know it's gonna take more than that, right?"

"Really?" I asked skeptically.

Her response was to grab my boxers and sweats, allowing me to step into them before she pulled them up to rest right below my balls. Looking at me again, she took my dick firmly in her hand and began to slowly massage it.

"DJ, I'm not like these other bitches," she whispered. "Good dick is only a bonus, it's not the whole package. And do you know why, DJ? Do you?"

I wanted to answer, but she had me rock hard in her hands and she was stroking it faster now. I could feel the need building within me and I reached out to pull her into my arms, but she took just a tiny step back.

"Answer me, DJ. Do you know why it just can't be about this good, big, black dick you got?"

"Uh-uh," I mumbled.

Then she did something that turned me on even more: she spit in her hand and went right back to pulling on my dick. bringing the feel of her delicate fingers on my shaft to life in a way I'd never known.

"Listen closely, baby, because I don't wanna have to say this again," she whispered, stepping toward me just a little.

I could hear her, but the roaring in my ears was getting louder, and I knew what was coming. *Me.*

"Bri-Brianna! I'ma. I'ma."

"Stay focused, DJ, and listen to me."

"I'm list-listening!"

"It's about more than dick because *dick don't last.*"

Suddenly she stopped stroking and squeezed the head of my dick before bending to kiss it softly. That kiss sent me over the edge, and not a second too soon did she swing my dick to the right, and I shot an avalanche of cum across the room. Even before I finished cumming I felt my knees weaken, and I was forced to lean on the bed or fall.

I'm not sure how long I remained in that position, but when I regained my wits, she was standing next to me with a shit-eating grin on her face and eyes that sparkled hazel-green.

"Who-who are you?" I panted, knowing I'd met my match in more ways than one.

"For now I'm your friend, but once you love me, who knows what I'll be," she replied, placing a quick kiss on my lips and grabbing the guns before heading toward the door.

"Where are you going?"

"Oh, you can handle it from here. I'll meet you out front."

And with that she left me right there, dick out, ass out, damn near spaced out. It took me ten long minutes to pull myself together and make it out front, where I found her seated behind the wheel of my car, puffing on a blunt.

"Where'd you find the keys?" I asked, sliding into the passenger seat.

"In the ignition where you left them. Here, hit this and it should make you feel better."

I took the offered blunt and inhaled the strawberry Kush as she pointed us in the direction of my house. I had a feeling this woman was full of surprises, but I wasn't sure if that was a good thing or bad thing yet. Once the weed took ahold of me, I turned on my music and listened to that old Kevin Gates *John Gotti*, feeling untouchable and like my dope boy ambitions could have my full attention after the funeral.

I'd mourn the loss of my father forever, but he'd raised me to be a great man, and most of the great men who shaped history were criminals first. In my mind I was history in the making.

"DJ?"

"Huh?"

"Cops."

"Behind us?" I asked, checking my side mirror, but not seeing anything.

"No, there," she replied, and that's when I realized we were coming up the driveway to the main house.

What I saw sobered me up really quickly, because there was a cop car, ambulance, and a coroner's van, which meant somebody was definitely dead on the premises.

"My house," I told her, needing to know what was going on before I walked into it. We pulled into the garage and I shut the door behind us.

"What do you think happened?" she asked me.

"No clue. Come on, let's go in and hopefully somebody is down here to tell us what the fuck is going on."

It took me a while to make my way into the house, and when I got to my living room I got my second shock in ten minutes.

"What the fuck, JuJu?" I yelled, coming into my living room to see her sitting on my couch while there was a half-conscious, naked bitch bleeding on my floor.

"Okay, it looks bad, but I can explain," she replied quickly. "See, we were—"

"That's Ruby," Brianna said from beside me.

"Who?" I asked.

"Ruby, Tae's right hand."

"Bri, help me," she slurred, blood leaking from several spaces in her mouth.

"Okay, wait! JuJu, tell me what happened," I said.

"Me and baby were working on her when CJ runs in the house screaming Belinda killed herself."

"She did what?" I asked in disbelief.

"She shot herself in the head. CJ tried to save her and called the paramedics, but—"

"Where's my daughter?" Bri asked.

"Upstairs sleeping. She's fine."

"Belinda killed herself?" I asked again, still not believing it.

"Yeah. She left a note saying without your dad there was no need to live. Some real Romeo and Juliet type shit," JuJu said.

With that statement I knew there was more blood and another life on my hands and conscious. Belinda was a great woman and she'd been the best stepmother she could to me, even though she hadn't had to. She'd loved me like I was hers. And I killed her, too.

"Where's Deshana?" I asked.

"At the main house, dealing with everything and keeping them from coming this way."

"Okay, well, we gotta clean this shit up. Kill this bitch already and get her body far and away from here," I ordered, heading toward my office.

"Uh, there's a slight problem with that," JuJu replied.

"Bri, please. Please help me," Ruby begged.

"What problem?" I asked.

"She's pregnant."

The look I gave JuJu asked if I really had to make all the hard decisions, but Brianna spoke before I could.

"Who's is it?"

"Bri, please!" she moaned, coughing up more blood and what looked like teeth.

"Who's is it, Ruby?"

"It's–it's Tae's, but—"

"So you were fucking him, huh?"

"It's not like that, it was never like that."

"Yeah, that's what you said the whole time, bitch! But it's lies. All of it was lies!" she screamed.

Before me stood a woman I didn't know, but she was definitely introducing herself to the world in this moment.

"Bri," I said, trying to get her to look at me instead of focusing her hate-filled gaze on the helpless woman on my floor. "Brianna."

"You two deserve each other, and since he's dead, bitch, guess what that means for you!"

"Brianna!" I yelled again, but now she had a pistol in her hand and she was moving toward her.

"This ain't you, Bri. This ain't how you wanna live the rest of your life," I warned her.

She paused for a minute just to look at me, and I saw her heart breaking right before my eyes. I didn't think even she realized how much she still loved Tae until that moment.

"This is me, DJ. And this is what I want."

Before I could say another word, she pulled the trigger.

Aryanna

Chapter Nine

DJ

The clicking of the safety preventing her from firing a bullet into Ruby's brain gave me time to get to her and take the gun away. I didn't think I was strong enough to keep wrestling with her, though, so once I had the gun I turned her loose.

"She deserves to die!" Brianna screamed in my face before her overwhelming emotions forced her to run from the room.

This being Devonte's right hand meant she deserved to die, but that child had no one to speak for it. Brianna couldn't see it now, but for all intents and purposes she'd been Ruby.

So what if it hadn't been me? Both her and little Hope would be beyond this world, and my soul would be damned beyond any higher beings' ability to cleanse it. In this world there were very few things that separated man from animal. In my opinion, sometimes it was just one decision at a time.

"Get her out of my house, JuJu, but don't kill her!"

"What am I supposed to do with her?"

"Right now put her stinking ass in a bath, and we'll figure it out once Deshana gets back. And get rid of this gun; it's dirty."

Tossing her the pistol, I left her to handle Ruby while I went to find Bri and hopefully talk some sense into her. My chest was hurting like a muthafucka and I could see spots of red through the hospital gown, which meant I'd opened something. All I could do was hope it wasn't bad, because I damn sure wasn't going back to the hospital.

I got to the top of the stairs and started to go left to where Brianna's room was, but I heard the sounds of her crying from my room. When I opened the door I found her sprawled on the floor, this time clutching the pearl-handled .38 I kept in my nightstand. I prayed she hadn't gone completely bat shit, because this gun had no safety and it packed a punch like Evander "The Real Deal" Holyfield.

"Bri," I said cautiously, closing my bedroom door as I entered the room.

At first she just lay there crying, and I wasn't sure she heard me, but as I got closer she turned her tear-stained face my way. So much pain filled her eyes, but even in this moment she possessed a beauty unlike any woman I'd ever known. I could see her strength even now, as clearly as I could see she didn't wanna be strong. In this moment she needed something and someone more than herself, and I understood the realization of what she'd almost done had hit home.

"Come here," I told her, opening my arms, holding her close as she clung to me tightly.

I had no idea and no way of knowing what hurts she'd had to endure in her life, but I knew this one was a major one not to be forgotten soon. I'd heard everything she said to me in the hospital, but one thing I knew with absolute certainty was good dick could make you forget for a while.

Pulling back just a little, I captured her soft lips with my own, my kiss asking for permission as much as it was seeking knowledge of her. Our tongues danced like old friends with the understanding new lovers have of things never being the same after that moment. We clawed at each other's clothing until all that could be felt was flesh upon flesh, our heartbeats racing as two sets of lungs became one.

"I want you,' I panted in between kisses.

"Then take me," she replied, grabbing my dick and leading me to the bed.

I wanted to blow her back out, but already I could hear my body screaming its limitations, and so I elected to do something I had yet to give a woman: intimacy.

"Close your eyes."

"What?"

"Close your eyes and trust me," I told her, kissing her closed eyelids before covering the rest of her face with kisses.

I let my lips burn a trail along her jaw line and down her neck as I slowly turned her around until her plump, juicy ass was backed right up against my dick. Using one hand to take her ponytail down, I allowed the other to roam freely over her luscious curves while I continued kissing across her shoulder blades.

I could feel her body come alive and talk to me, whispering its secrets like they were mine to keep forever. Pulling her closer, I used both hands to cup her breasts, my lips and tongue now walking along her spine, and I felt the shiver of anticipation. I lay on the bed and pulled her to me so we fit together like spoons, feeling our heartbeats synchronize.

"It's just me and you," I whispered in her ear, loving the steady throb coming from her pussy as I rubbed my dick across her slippery, wet lips. Gently I pushed inside her, taking my time until we fit together like a hand and glove.

"DJ," she whispered.

"I got you, baby, just trust me." Lacing our fingers, I brought our joined hands to her breasts, allowing us to both play with her nipples while I set the pace of our dance.

Each time I pulled out, her wetness sucked me back in and allowed me to explore deeper, forcing the breath from my lungs as her pussy held me in a loving vice grip. I could feel her body calling out to my own, demanding savage attention, but I knew we both needed more than the physical. We needed love.

In that moment, time stood still, it really was just us, and we gave each other everything until there was nothing left.

"DJ, baby, I'm cumming. I'm-I'm cumming!"

"Me too, baby," I replied pounding inside her until all I could see was a brilliant white light, and I felt her delicious juices rain all over me. Neither of us moved, and for the first time in my life I didn't wanna be anywhere except where I was with this woman.

"DJ?"

"Hmm?"

"Have you ever made love before?"

"Nah, I don't think so, why?"

"Neither have I, but I think that's what it feels like," she replied softly.

"So you love me, huh?" I asked, smiling.

"Asked and answered," she said, and I could hear the smile in her voice.

We lay there just like that until the intercom went off, summoning me to the living room.

"Now what?" I wondered aloud.

"Probably your sister. Hold on, let me clean your chest first," she said, getting out of bed and going into the bathroom.

I lay there admiring the view of her firm ass, hoping we had so much more to do in this bedroom. As cliché as it sounded, I really had never known a woman like her before, especially not one who fit into my future plans. Every king needed a queen, though.

"Lay on your back," she ordered, sitting on the bed next to me with a first aid kit.

"Do you know what you're doing?"

"Guess we'll have to find out, now won't we," she replied, smiling seductively.

"Be gentle."

"Not hardly, but don't worry, you'll like it rough."

We continued our flirtatious banter as she cleaned and redressed my wounds, but sooner than I'd like she was done.

"Put some clothes on and meet me downstairs."

"Okay, but I need to check on Hope first. I feel like I haven't seen my baby in forever."

"Give her a kiss for me."

"I can do that, but what are you gonna do for me?"

My actions spoke for me, pulling her toward me for a kiss full of passionate promise. I could feel that hunger for her building again, but before we could fully explore it the intercom started blaring again for me to come downstairs.

"To be continued?" I asked hopeful.

Her response was to grab ahold of my rock-hard dick and take it all the way to the back of her throat while looking at me, slurping at the flavors of our lovemaking. And just as quickly she was up and headed out the door, laughing at the pained expression on my face and I'm sure the comedy of me flat on my back with my dick saluting.

"That's just wrong!" I yelled after her.

As quickly as my injuries allowed, I put on some shorts and a t-shirt before making my way back downstairs, where I walked into the same scene I left with one additional person.

"Please tell me why this bitch is still bleeding on my floor?" I asked, looking from JuJu to my sister.

"Where you been, DJ?" Deshana asked.

"Dealing with Brianna, but I told—"

"Fuck what you told anybody!" she roared, jumping to her feet. "I've been dealing with cops and their questions, not to mention a bitch so goddamn hysterical she had to be sedated, and you're getting your dick wet? You're just like your damn daddy, but guess what, my nigga? You ain't him!"

"I never said I was, but—"

"Don't come with no lame-ass excuse, because we don't do that. If you're a man, then admit when you're wrong."

"Okay, you're right, and I'm wrong! Happy now?" I yelled back at her.

I didn't like how she was coming at me like I was some little kid, even if she was right to an extent. I hadn't gone upstairs with sex on my mind, it kinda just happened. Either way, I was grown! And I didn't have to explain myself.

"You just don't get it, do you?" she asked, shaking her head in frustration.

"Get what, Deshana? What am I missing?" I saw that look in her eyes and knew something bad was coming.

"JuJu," she said, holding her hand out, and JuJu handed her the pistol I'd given her earlier. The same .44 DE that had ended my father's life.

"Who are you?" she asked, flipping the safety off and chambering a round into the head.

"What? Quit playin'," I replied uneasily.

"Does it look like I am playin', li'l nigga. I asked you a question."

"You know who I am. I'm your fucking brother."

"Really? And what's your name?" she asked, now standing over Ruby.

"You know my name."

"Yeah, I know your name, but do you know your name?"

It was on the tip of my tongue to tell her to quit playin' again, but the gleam in her eye said this was as serious as it got.

"I'm-I'm DJ."

"You don't sound too sure of that, li'l bruh. Who. The fuck. Are you?"

"What's going on?" Brianna asked, walking into the room with the baby in her arms. The tension was so thick she didn't dare to ask the question twice, but Deshana only spared her the briefest glance.

"I'm DJ," I said forcefully.

"And what's DJ stand for?" Deshana asked, gripping the pistol tighter.

"I'm Devaughn Junior."

"You're Devaugh Mitchell Junior?" she asked, cocking her head as she looked at me.

"Yeah."

As soon as the word left my mouth, she pulled the trigger and blew the top of Ruby's skull off. I felt Brianna jump beside me as little Hope let loose massive screams from the noise, but my eyes were locked on my sister, who was walking toward me.

"Act like it then, nigga. We put our own work in around here," she said, stopping in front of me.

I was speechless, completely caught up in the cold fury in her eyes, because for the first time I was seeing all of my big sister, and that terrified me.

"When you're man enough to make the really ugly decisions, then you're man enough to give orders in this family. Until then, you might want to think about what it means to be Devaughn Mitchell Junior, because my daddy was a helluva nigga. Let's go, Ju," she said, dropping the pistol at my feet as her and her wife walked out the front door. I couldn't put into words what I just witnessed, but I knew it was something I'd never forget.

"DJ, she just. I mean, she just."

"I know. Take Hope upstairs until I can get someone to clean this up."

"But DJ, if she ever finds out, we're dead."

"Trust me, if she ever finds out, death will be the best possible outcome," I said, going to my office and closing the door behind me.

In all the years I had spent in school, I'd never gotten the lessons I'd learned in the last five minutes. Algebraic equations be damned; the math was much simpler than that. My father had been number one, and I thought me being junior made me number two, but I was wrong. Deshana Mitchell was number two, and she was both as uncompromising and uncaring as my namesake had been.

"System online. Code word Judas," I said, ordering my computers to go operational. It was time to get back to work. Obvious my sister played chess on a clock.

"3-D Facetime, Mad Hacker."

Moments later his face appeared next to my computer monitor. "You ok, DJ?" he asked.

"How much did you see?"

"A-All of it! But I erased it from the hospital database."

"And?"

"What am I supposed to say? You don't pay me to question your reasoning."

"You're right, I don't. I've got big shoes to fill now, so it's time to get to work."

"Tell me where to start."

I let this thought turn over in my mind for a while, trying to get a feel for what my first move should be.

"I want all of Harley's formulas verified for our operation, and then I wanna know who's dealing what in this part of the world. We'll meet with them after the funeral. I want you to give my sister and her people whatever tech support they need to complete the takeover of New York City, and then I want background on everybody who is a big deal when it comes to gangbanging from Rhode Island to Florida and over into Texas. We'll meet with them around the same time. And I want what's left of the team here before the funeral to pay their last respects to a great man."

"What about your legal situation?"

"I'm out on a million-dollar bond and everything should work out smoothly. If it doesn't, we go to plan B."

"As in?"

"Evy, you know exactly what plan B is."

I couldn't tell if the look in his eyes was fear or respect, but either way he understood at this point in my life there was no one I wouldn't kill.

"Anything else?" he asked.

"Yeah, Tory is gonna get with you about my dad's money and businesses."

"She's already working on it. So far we're up to twelve billion in legal money and assets. Do you have time to go over some stuff?"

"Let's do it. Oh, and find someone to come clean up my houses real quick. It's been a long day."

From that point we worked on into the night, going over what my father owned and what his will specified he wanted done. It seemed like he knew his wife might not live long after him, because he'd put Deshana in charge of most of the businesses. Unless by some miracle Ramona woke up, because then she controlled everything except the money he'd been specific about.

Thinking about her reminded me of the phone call I had to make to inform them of what had happened. Given the late hour, I opted for an email instead. Once that task was complete, I made my way to bed where I found Brianna lying there, looking wide-eyed at the dome over the ceiling. We didn't talk and we didn't make love; we fucked in fear of what the future might bring down on us.

We both understood that there was no going back on the decisions we'd made, so for better or worse we were in it together. In the days leading up to the funeral we tried to find a routine of normalcy, but we both understood it could all be for nothing. Our fate depended upon our ability to keep the light out of the darkness, because in the darkness death consumes us all.

Aryanna

Chapter Ten

Ramona

It had taken four days after I woke up in hell and was taken off the pulsating muscle stimulation machines for my doctor to agree I was okay to fly, and his agreement only came after I threatened to knee cap him. These had been the longest ninety-six hours of my life filled with unspeakable joy at the wonder that was my Isabella, yet equally unspeakable pain at the loss we'd both suffered. How could Devaughn be dead, and by the hands of his own child, no less?

But then again, the man I loved and remembered would willingly give his life for any of his children, no matter the circumstances. I longed for his touch, but all I had were very few memories to keep me warm now. Still, they were cherished.

The fact Isabella had gotten to know and love her father was a source of great comfort, because I'd feared it would never come to pass. It wasn't easy seeing the pain in my baby's eyes over her loss, and it broke my heart how much like the both of us she was. My sass and his thoughtful analysis were a sight to be seen, and I prayed wherever he was that he was watching over us.

I also prayed he'd keep my pistol steady, because he knew I wouldn't feel right until I had some of his enemy's blood on my hands. According to my father, he'd pulled quite a coup, but I wasn't surprised because his ability to really see the chessboard is what kept him alive for as long as it had.

I was channeling him in that aspect now, because I knew just because the queen fell didn't mean the game was over. Until I was satisfied no one who ever posed him a threat still existed, I was determined to bring all the pain in my power.

"When will you leave?" my father asked, coming up behind me on the balcony.

"The funeral is in a few more days. I need to be there and in place before then."

"You understand why I cannot allow you to go on this journey by yourself?"

"Do you understand why it can't be you who goes with me?" I asked, turning to look at him.

As a parent I understood his protective instincts, and the truth of the matter was thirteen years' unconsciousness had given my body time to betray me. My panic at not being able to use my legs was not as short-lived as I'd hoped, but the doctor assured me the damage wasn't permanent. I was determined to give my all to physical therapy, but first there were wrongs that had to be righted.

"I understand you see me as but an old fool, but I am more."

"Papa, you are nobody's fool, and you never will be. As for age, you don't look a day over fifty," I said, giving him a wink.

"Your kindness warms my heart, truly. You have to understand, though, the last time I left you alone to handle business, this is how you came back to me," he said, gesturing toward the wheelchair I was sitting in.

It was useless to argue with him and better to reach a compromise we could both live with.

"What is it you propose, Papa?"

"You mean aside from the army you will travel with and the friends of ours to meet you on American soil?"

"If I thought this was all you had planned, I'd readily agree," I told him, smiling and knowing him better than that.

"It is true I do have one other request, but I must preface it with an explanation."

"Okay," I replied warily.

"For years I was forced to live with the tragedy of what happened to you, never knowing if you would one day awaken or if you were in any pain. Constantly questioning if I was simply being selfish and stubborn by keeping you alive. And even while enduring this, I had the task of constant vigilance over Isabella, fearing every moment she was out of my sight even though her own father loved her beyond reproach. From the time she was but a toddler, I understood I must be prepared for anything to arise in her life, whether it be past or future troubles. And the only way for me to be comfortable and fully prepared was to prepare her."

Taking a moment to let his words digest, I tried to quiet the rumblings of apprehension in the pit of my stomach.

"Dad, what are you saying?"

"Perhaps it would be simpler for me to show you," he said, stepping to the railing of the balcony and looking down.

"Isabella! Demonstrate!" he bellowed in Italian.

Rolling slowly to the railing, I looked down into the garden, and what I saw froze me in place. On one side of the garden were several bottles lined up along a low back wall. About one hundred feet away stood my beautiful baby girl with an equally beautiful pistol clutched in her grip.

"Oh no," I mumbled, but before I could protest she leveled the all-black I-911 .45 and fired five quick shots with her right hand. She then proceeded to switch hands and fire five more, reducing all the bottles to nothing more than dust.

But she wasn't done. Turning and taking off at a dead run between the rows of orange and lemon trees, she fired round after round at targets that were strategically set up, moving almost as if she was invisible.

And she knew her gun, because never once did I hear the dry clicking of an empty chamber. When every target was hit, some more than once, she stepped back out of the rows and looked expectantly toward my father, who in turn looked to me.

"Papa, what have you done?" I whispered, completely shocked at what I'd just witnessed.

"I taught her to defend herself."

"But she's. She's just a child! An innocent child!" I screamed.

"Impossible," he replied in Italian.

"What?"

"You're her mother, and Devaughn is her father, so the word *innocent* will never apply to her!" he replied vigorously. "Now, we can be naïve about that and hope for the best, or we can prepare her for the cold world that you chose to bring her into. Have you already forgotten that you're a made woman? One day to be Capo Di Tutt'i Capi?"

The truth was I had forgotten. With everything else going on that honor kind of slipped my mind, but even with that fact it was still hard to process what I just saw.

"Bella!" I yelled, summoning my daughter to me.

"Do not scold her, she has only done what I taught her to do. I apologize if you feel as if I have overstepped, but I did what I thought right in this situation. We cannot control the world and how it will turn, so the best we can do is prepare ourselves for what comes with this life of chaos."

And with that he left me to talk to my little girl, who had just rushed onto the balcony.

"Yes, Mama?" she asked, hands behind her back.

What could I say? How could I argue the truth of my father's words when it had been my own selfish and deliberate decision to get pregnant? The truth was I had killed, and I would probably kill again. The truth was my baby's father, my husband and the love of my life, was a killer at heart. That didn't make us bad people. It was just the world we lived in, and the one she'd been born into.

"Where is your pistol?" I asked.

Slowly she pulled her hands from behind her, but her face was a mask of uncertainty. The gun looked so out of place in my sweet, innocent little girl's hands that it broke my heart, but the harsh reality was my tears wouldn't save her life one day.

"You can't take that with us when we leave, do you understand?"

"Yes, Mama."

"You understand why we're going back?"

"For my daddy's funeral."

"It may be more than that though, baby, because both mommy and daddy have enemies there," I explained patiently, wondering where this conversation was in the parenting handbook.

"I understand. Daddy always told me real family protects each other."

Hearing her speak about life lessons learned from Devaughn brought instant tears to my eyes, but I was determined not to let them fall.

"Your daddy was right. Now, I want you to put your pistol away and start packing, because we leave soon."

"Okay, Mama. But...."

"What is it, sweetheart?"

"Did I do good?"

I had to smile at this, because it was the perfectionist in me she inherited. "You did wonderful," I replied, opening my arms for a hug, which she eagerly gave me.

After inhaling her childlike smell with its mixture of gunpowder, I let her go so I could gather my thoughts. There would never come a moment when I'd regret my decision to get pregnant because I had made that decision out of love. But was

I selfish? Had I only considered my feelings and happiness in the matter with complete disregard for the life I was bringing my daughter into? These were questions I knew would haunt me until my days' end, and probably beyond when I was forced to watch my daughter struggle to survive in a world not of her making. For today I took comfort in the fact she was alive and well.

I felt my father's presence even though he didn't speak, and I knew he didn't deserve my anger. "Will she ever forgive me for bringing her into this world, into this life?" I whispered.

"Have you forgiven me, my love?" he replied softly.

Turning toward him, I was shocked to see a look of uncertainty on my father's face.

"Papa, there has never been anything to forgive. I've had a great life full of love and many treasured memories, and you have always gone above and beyond to keep me safe and happy. What more could I ask for?"

"But I could not protect you when it counted."

"Nonsense. What happened to me was not your fault, and I won't let you blame yourself. I am who I am because of you, which means we have no regrets. Understand?"

"I understand. And that means you needn't ask if your own daughter will forgive you, because she follows an example of unconditional love."

I felt the weight of self-doubt lift as he engulfed me in his strong arms and I inhaled the sweet smell of his cigar mixed with the olives he still loved to eat. Neither of us may be what anyone would ever consider perfect parents, but like the bible says, let he who is without sin cast the first stone.

"So, I assume your proposition is that I take Bella with me and keep her close at all times," I said, sitting back in my wheelchair.

"It is a deceptively good plan, is it not?"

"But there is a difference between targets and real people, Papa. You must understand that."

The look in his eyes told me there was something I didn't know, and I felt the hairs rise on the back of my neck.

"During this latest battle of Devaughn's, Isabella was in the states for quite some time. She has seen death," he informed me regretfully.

"That doesn't mean she can dish it out, though," I argued.

He gave me the saddest smile before opening his mouth to speak again. "She has the blood of a Sicilian. She will avenge her family when the time comes."

I understood right then he hadn't simply taught Isabella to shoot, he'd submerged her in the culture and essence that was Sicily. The Sicilian will to fight went all the way back to the slave revolt against the Romans in 132 B.C., and I'd learned that at my father's knee. I didn't have to imagine what my daughter was capable of because I knew. She was born with the blood of a Don, to say nothing of her father's royal bloodline.

"Tell me everything I need to know before we go back there," I said.

By the time he'd finished bringing me up to speed on the wars and causalities, as well as updating me on the business side of things, the sun was once again retreating for the night and I felt like my mind would explode. It seemed that from the time Devaughn woke up, he never stopped fighting, but he was always smarter than his opponent and knew how to adapt.

I could only admit to myself how much it hurt to hear of him taking another wife, but the evidence it was truly love was in the fact it was now a double funeral. I didn't feel like his love of her could take away from the love we shared though, and part of me respected that he had the courage to go on losing so much. I couldn't imagine how he felt after losing me, Candy, and Latavia all in the same night after losing five years of his own life.

A weaker man would have been broken beyond repair, but not my man. Despite his relationship status, he'd always be my man. I was grateful to my father for keeping a constant visual over the man who meant the world to me, and for understanding he couldn't have interfered without Devaughn asking for help.

I still needed an inside view, and I knew Deshana would be the only one who could give me what I needed. It was still hard to believe DJ, sweet little DJ, was for all intents and purposes the new king. And he was involved in shit not even Devaughn would do? I definitely had to have a sit down with him A.S.A.P.!

The one thing that troubled me was how Devaughn had allowed his mother to live. I understood killing ones' parents was an unspeakable form of treason, but I knew my husband and his love for me. So, did the fact he let her live mean I had to do the same?

"You said Devonte was raised in New York by his grandmother?" I asked, knowing I had to tread lightly because my father was under the impression Keyz shot me.

"Yes, by Devaughn's mother. And the Bloods."

"Did Devaughn ever visit?"

"No, and she never stepped foot back in Virginia, either. Until."

I appreciated my dad's sensitivity to the topic of my husband being murdered, but I was aligning the rest of the pieces of the puzzle. The way it sounded was like he banished both of them as if they never existed, which would've been his way of showing mercy. Devonte may have been dead, but I didn't have any intentions on being merciful with the woman I'd once thought an ally.

"Mama, will you come down and have dinner with me?" Isabella asked, breaking my train of thought.

"Of course, sweetheart, we'll be down in a minute. Send one of the guards up," I replied.

"Ok."

"Do you have all the information you require?" my father asked.

"I think so. Anything else I can find out from Deshana."

"A ruthless one, she is," he replied, shaking his head in approval.

"Trust me, I remember when she was but a few years older than Bella. Deadly, with great instincts, too. I'm looking forward to seeing her."

"It'll be a surprise, to say the least. Tell me, why did you not want me to mention it to DJ when I communicated Bella would attend the service?"

"I admit I have an agenda, but mainly I have questions, and I didn't have time for rehearsed answers," I replied honestly.

"Do you not trust his family?"

"In a family where your own sister rapes you, gets pregnant, and that child in turn is the one who takes your life, would you trust anyone?"

"Touché."

"There are more secrets, and I intend to find out what they are."

Aryanna

Chapter Eleven

Devonte

"Push! Come one, you gotta push, Tae!" she screamed in my ear.

I wanted to slap the shit out of her little ass, but I barely had enough strength to fight the weight I was lifting.

"Two more, come on!"

"That's. What you. You said four reps ago!" I yelled back.

"If you can talk, you can rep! Four more!"

I wouldn't think by looking at Tiffany's tiny frame that she would be some workout nut, but the bitch was loco! Nobody wanted me to recover faster than I did, but she was pushing me like her life depended on it.

"Okay, that's good," she said, taking the ten-pound weight from my sore and trembling arm.

The cannon DJ shot me with tore my shit up pretty bad, but it wasn't beyond repair. And I was determined.

"Good workout."

"Shit, easy for you to say, all you did was yell at me," I panted, taking a long drink from the water bottle she passed me.

"It's not yelling, it's motivation. And besides, Amber didn't complain as much as you."

This comment caused laughter to come from the back porch a few feet away. We'd only been out of the hospital a few days, but as soon as the challenge was understood and accepted, Tiffany had turned the backyard into her own personal boot camp from hell. It wasn't just about strengthening our bodies from the gunshot wounds, she was training us.

"Shit ain't funny, Amber," I replied sourly.

"What, I didn't say nothing!" she said innocently.

"And why do we gotta do all this while he's in there yelling about a damn war Eagle touchdown?" I asked.

"Well, because my husband works hard and he deserves his down time. Plus, that is Alabama playing Auburn, and if me running around the house butt naked ain't moving him from in front of the game, then nothing will," Tiffany replied.

I took a moment to just look at her and admire the way her spandex was hugging her curves. Then I tried to envision her naked.

"Stop looking at me like that, negro, we family."

And here I thought I was getting away with something because it was getting dark outside.

"He nasty like that," Amber said, laughing again.

"Uh-huh, just like his...."

I knew what she was gonna say, but it was still kinda hard to think of myself having a father. The streets, my homies, and my grandma were all I'd ever known for real, especially after my mom disappeared. Now I had the shadow of this "legend" to try to process, but there was still so much hate in my heart for all he'd done.

"How well did you know Devaughn?" I asked Tiffany.

"Uh, well, your uncle and me have been together since we were kids, so I think I met him when he was about fourteen years old."

"And?"

"And what?"

"What was he like?"

She laughed before she answered.

"Honestly, that boy was bad as hell, but he had a good heart."

"Yeah, right."

"No, for real. Okay, I remember this time he stole some weed from your uncle. It wasn't much, probably like thirty dollars' worth. But he did it so he could buy his girlfriend a fleece from old navy.

"Aw," Amber exclaimed.

"Or I remember how he use to come by the hospital all the time and ask me if I needed money for lunch, just to check on me because we were family."

"He doesn't sound like the badass Devaughn Mitchell," I replied.

"Oh there're other stories about his robberies, kidnappings, and shootings, but the point I'm making is deep down he wasn't a bad person. He just did bad things."

"So, what happened?"

"Prison happened. It changed him, made him colder. Not to mention that gang shit he got caught up in. We never did understand that because he was so much smarter than that decision, but he'd found something he was good at. He could've been anything, but I think he chose to be the bad guy because it's what everyone expected him to be."

"Including you?" Amber asked.

"Actually, no. I expected him to learn from others' mistakes and make the most of the second chance he was given."

"Why do you think he didn't?" I asked, curious now.

"Because he felt he had to right too many wrongs. He came out with only revenge on his mind, and that consumed him."

"So then, he should've just let it go and moved on with his life?" Amber asked.

"Sometimes you can't let it go. Sometimes it's worth whatever the cost," I said, understanding on a deeper level what drove a man I didn't even know.

Tiffany just looked at me, but I didn't know if she was seeing me or the boy she used to know. Maybe it was both.

"I knew your mom, too, you know." Tiffany said.

This got my attention immediately.

"How?"

"She used to live with us. It was actually me and your uncle who took her to see your father all those years ago, but of course we couldn't see this coming."

"What was she like?" I asked softly, knowing I was quite possibly getting ready to fall down the rabbit hole.

"To tell you the truth, she was lost. When your grandfather died, her whole world changed dramatically. He was all she really had because her mom wasn't shit. She was at that age where she needed the right type of attention from a male figure, but all she was getting were dudes trying to get what she had between her legs."

"Including my father."

"I didn't know about that. They were friends, but I don't think she needed him to be her friend. She needed guidance and structure. Their friendship allowed her to see him as a man instead of who he truly was. Ultimately, I'd say what happened was both of their faults."

"But he was grown, right?" Amber asked.

"Age doesn't make you grown. He was an adult in years of age, but he'd been doing time since he was fifteen, so how much growing had he actually done on a mature level? And who were his examples and role models? I'm not making excuses, but I don't want either of you painting this portrait in your mind of a black and white scenario. Life is fucked up; some survive it, some don't."

Her words gave me a lot to think about. To hear from her about who my parents had been versus what the streets had to say was a different kind of education. The street tales makes them legends, but Tiffany's words made them human. I doubted DJ ever really knew the man he called dad. Maybe no one did.

"Are we finished for the night? I'ma take a shower and get some sleep," I said.

"Yeah, we're done. It'll be harder tomorrow, though," she warned.

This got a moan of dread from Amber that made me smile, because at least I wouldn't be in pain alone. I made my way past my uncle and grandma who were glued to the T.V, and upstairs to the bathroom for a hot shower. After years of living like royalty and spending money faster than the cashier could say 'credit or debit,' it felt hella weird to be in what some would call a "normal" house.

I felt like I was in a show box! When I'd made the suggestion we go to a hotel or buy a house down there, I was reminded dead men did neither of those things. Then I was told how spoiled I was as my aunt and uncle proceeded to tell me about their meager upbringings in Reston, Virginia. Like that was my fault! I had to admit the house parties and the go-gos sounded like something I could get behind, if the house was big enough.

Turning on the shower, I stripped out of the sweatpants and t-shirt I had on and was just about to get naked when Amber came through the door, naked.

"Is the water hot?" she asked.

"I don't know, I'll let you know once I get out," I replied, smiling.

"Very funny, smartass."

Before I had a chance to say anything else, she was standing in front of me, giving me a devilish grin to match the twinkle in her eyes.

"Amber."

"Don't make this weird," she said, pulling the shower curtain back and stepping beneath the spray.

A million thoughts went through my mind, but I said fuck 'em all as I got naked and followed her lead.

"Wash my back," she ordered, handing me a bar of soap.

I took the soap and began making small circles on her back, already wondering how far down to go. When I got to the dip in her spine right above her ass, she turned around.

"Now wash my front."

I let my fingers walk along the reddish-purple welts from where the buckshot had hit her in the side, allowing my mind to flash back to that night just a short time ago. I could feel myself coming to life, remembering how it felt to be inside her.

"Hold this," I said, passing her the soap after lathering my hands thoroughly.

Taking both her titties in my hands I began to caress her slowly, loving the sight of the fire building in her eyes. Before I knew it she had her own hands full of soap and she was gently stroking my dick to the same rhythm that I was using on her nipples.

"That's enough playing," I said, pulling her toward me, kissing her hard enough to bruise her succulent lips.

She returned in kind, grabbing my dick like it belonged to her and stroking it faster. I knew my arm wouldn't allow me to lift her, but I had to be inside her. Now!

Spinning her around, I grabbed a fistful of her hair as I bent her under the water spray and shoved my dick inside her tight, warm pussy with enough force to have her on her tiptoes.

"Oh! Oh God," she moaned, using her hands to brace herself against the wall while I pounded her with purpose-driven strokes.

The heat of the water was no match for what I was feeling inside her, and I could feel her body rocking with the wave of her first orgasm.

"Shit," I mumbled, feeling the mysteries of her unfold as she clenched her pussy around my dick.

I wanted to cum, but this was a battle of wills, and I refused to accept defeat. No sooner had the first wave passed when I started feeding her longer strokes, trying to tickle her ribs with the force of every one.

"Tae, don't-don't, oh fuck! Don't s-s-stop!" she screamed, skin slapping loudly sounding more like hand-to-hand combat than sex.

I rode her hard, loving how she arched her back and threw her tight little ass back at me. When I stuck my thumb in her asshole, I thought she was gonna hop head first into the wall, but the increased wetness of her throbbing pussy told me her secrets.

Pulling out of one hole, I slowly worked my way inside her ass until she had all she could take, and then we began the dance again. I could feel it building in my toes, and with every stroke I felt us knocking on Heaven's door.

"Amber. Amber, I-oh shit!"

"Fuck me harder," she demanded.

I gave and she took, and we crumbled under intense climaxes, gasping for air that scorched our lungs. Sitting down in the shower while the water rained on us, I held her as we tried to find the axis the earth rotated on. I couldn't remember any experience so raw with power and passion, and I definitely didn't expect it from this small package.

"You-you were holding back in the hotel room, Ma," I panted.

"So were you," she replied, smiling up at me.

"Any more secrets I should know about?"

"So much more," she replied, pulling my lips to hers for a tender kiss.

Once I regained my strength, we set about the task of trying to bathe again, but somehow she ended up holding onto the shower rod while I devoured her whole. Of course, she couldn't be satisfied until she had me squirming and begging for mercy as she tried to suck the skin off of my dick.

"Are we gonna do this all night?"

"I don't think you can handle that yet," she replied, laughing and turning off the water. "Plus, you know what you gotta do."

I knew she was referring to the conversation I had to have with my grandmother, who was planning to attend her son's funeral tomorrow. I understood she felt she had to go, but I didn't think it was a smart move.

"Yeah, I know," I said, stepping out of the shower and grabbing a towel off the rack to dry off.

After I dried Amber off, we went across the hall to our temporary room where I threw on some shorts and a t-shirt before going to find my grandmother.

"Am I interrupting?" I asked her and my uncle, who were sitting on the back porch with their heads together, talking.

"This conversation involves you," she replied, making room for me to sit beside her.

"Are you really going?" I asked.

"He's my son, I owe him that, at least."

"Then I'm going with you."

"You know you can't do that, Tae."

"I'm not scared of DJ, or nobody else over there!" I said heatedly.

"Ain't about being scared, slim, it's about being smart," Maurice interjected.

I knew he was right. DJ still had an army and unlimited resources on his side, and I was hated now more than ever for something he'd done.

"Any news from up top?" I asked hopefully.

"None that's encouraging. Words like 'complete annihilation' are being used," she said.

"So, what's the plan?"

"Well, tomorrow I'm gonna watch them bury my son, and hopefully find out anything I can about your daughter. I'm definitely gonna have a conversation with Brianna."

"What good is that gonna do?" I saw a look between the both of them, but I wasn't sure what it meant.

"I'm gonna try to get her to admit to DJ shooting Devaughn and record it on my phone," my grandma said.

"We don't do no police shit."

"Stop talkin' sometimes and listen, young, damn!" Maurice exclaimed.

"I don't wanna record her for the cops. I'ma give it to someone who will change the game. I'ma give it to Deshana."

Aryanna

Chapter Twelve

Deshana

"Come in."

"What's crackin', big homie?"

"Shit, what's good, Ready Roc?"

"Yo, it's like a million fucking people out there already, and it's still lines of cars and shit."

"Yeah, I figured there would be. Pops was a big deal," I replied with a sad smile.

"But I'm saying, homie, it's news cameras and everything! I ain't never seen them celebrate or really give a fuck about a gang member. Look how they did Tookie after all the shit he did for the community; they still executed him."

"Yeah, I know, but it's different times now. And my dad wasn't a gang member, he was a gangster. They may never like it, but they gotta respect it, because he did it his way. He could've easily kept all of his money or gave it all to us, but taking care of the community and giving others a chance made him feel all the dirt he did wasn't just for the thrills."

"I feel that. Hopefully when it's my time to go I get the same love."

"Oh, don't misunderstand me, homie. It ain't all love. A lot of the muthafuckas just wanna make sure he's dead because they believed him to be the devil himself. Then you have some muthafuckas doing a temperature check to see if we're vulnerable in any way."

"I don't understand, then why open up the property like this and let them in?"

"Because when you know what's in your grass, you ain't gotta cut it. You just gotta make sure you look where you're stepping. Plus, this gives us a chance to see who's watching us."

"Genius," he replied, smiling and nodding his head.

I'd already known my father deserved the recognition. Would he have wanted it? No, but so many people had misconstrued opinions of him, and it didn't sit well with me. Although he never talked about it, I always knew what the label of a 'sex offender' did to his pride, especially since he hadn't been guilty. He'd done a lot of heinous shit, but he'd always known what would stick out in people's minds.

It never mattered to people criminals are creatures of habit, and no one could find a sex offense anywhere else in his past. All that mattered was what they thought they knew, but now they'd be forced to hear the whole story.

"Are you ready to perform?"

"Come on, homie. My name is Ready Roc, and performing is what I do."

I just stared at him for a minute so he could absorb the look on my face.

"A'ight, a'ight, a nigga might be a little nervous."

Now I laughed, because I could tell that when he was still commenting on how many people were out there.

"You'll be fine, plus DayDay will be out there with you," I assured him.

"About that."

"What?"

"Maybe you should holla at her."

I didn't like the sound of that shit at all. Sharday hadn't been even a shadow of herself since she'd come home and I'd broken the news to her, but the way she'd been acting had me worried. When I'd told her what happened, she'd simply shutdown, no tears or hysteria. She just went into herself like our mother had done all those years ago.

Thankfully she wasn't in a catatonic state, but if someone got more than ten-word conversation out of her, they were a bad muthafucka. I had almost put off my trip to New York, but JuJu and I had gotten up there and sewed shit up in under twenty-four hours. Now I was sitting in my father's office trying to get my bearings before the funeral got going, and here was another problem I didn't need.

"Where is she?" I asked.

"On the bus."

Her tour bus was parked behind the house, and it seemed like it was where she spent every single moment.

"A'ight, I'll go talk to her. In the meantime—"

I was interrupted by my phone going off, telling me I had a message.

"Message display," I ordered, watching as the 3-D image popped up showing a line of five black limos being stopped out front. The sight of limos wasn't anything out of the ordinary, but I knew my team had stopped them because they all had New York plates.

"I'm on my way," I said, slipping my phone back in my pocket and heading for the door.

"What do you want me to do about DayDay?" Ready called from behind me.

"Get her high and start rehearsing," I replied, still walking and trying to figure out who'd come from New York unannounced.

I knew it couldn't be any of my homies because the ones attending had flown back with me. And I knew with absolute certainty not a Blood alive would step foot on these premises, not unless he just really wanted to die that bad.

When I came out of the front doors, and started up the driveway, I saw what Ready Roc had been taking about. As far away as DJ's front yard ran, there were people everywhere. We'd had his body cremated and his ashes would be spread over D.C. by helicopter, but we'd still had a stage built and two symbolic coffins put in front of it. Belinda's family wanted their own private ceremony, but we still had to show our love.

There were rows upon rows of white lawn chairs spread out all over the grass, and from the looks of things there wouldn't be an empty seat. The plan was to have a brief period of mourning, at which time a few scriptures would be read and DayDay would perform the Faith Evans/P. Diddy collaboration *Missing You* with Ready Roc. After that it would be a party, because that was what the old man would've wanted.

Truthfully, what I wanted was for this day to be over, because none of this shit was gonna bring me my daddy back.

Approaching the first limo in the line, I touched the small of my back for the reassurance only my P89 Rugar gave me before I tapped on the passenger side window.

"Who's in the car?" I asked when the window slid down an inch.

"Second car," a voice said, and the window went right back up.

I really didn't have time for the bullshit today, but it wouldn't look good on the nightly news if I was seen spraying bullets at cars. Taking a deep breath, I walked all the way to the back of the second limo in line. Before I could knock on the door, it was opened and I was looking down into the face of my little sister, Bella.

"Hey, sweetheart, why didn't you just tell them it was you?" I asked, smiling at her.

"Get in," a familiar voice ordered, and Bella slid over to make room for me.

I only hesitated for a second, and then I climbed into the car, closing the door behind me. I gave my eyes time to adjust to the dark tint, but no amount of time could've prepared me for who was sitting across from me.

"Ra-Ramona," I said in disbelief.

She smiled and then took off the huge Dolce and Gabbana glasses covering her face.

"Oh my fucking God! Ramona!" I screamed, jumping across the car and into her open arms, squeezing her to be sure she was real.

"Bitch, what the fuck? How? When? How long?" I stammered, trying to get all my thoughts out at once.

"It's only been a few days, but I've missed you so much!" she replied, hugging me tightly. We've must've stayed like that for five minutes as our excitement gave way to tears, and then we just held onto each other, crying.

Very few people could understand what it was like, what this moment meant as a family, but Ramona got it. In some ways she'd suffered more because this was her third time around without him, yet it hadn't lessened her love in the slightest.

"Hold on," I said, pulling back so I could get to my phone.

"Message reply, last sender. Let all five cars in immediately," I ordered.

"Pretty tight security," she commented.

"Yeah, well, you know how that goes. God, I can't believe you're here! Dad would—"

"I know," she said, taking my hand as the car started up the driveway.

"When did you get back?" I asked.

"Only a few days ago, and I know I should've called immediately, but I had my reasons."

"Okay," I replied, waiting on her to elaborate.

"Thirteen years and so much has happened, Deshana, but there are things I don't understand."

I cut my eyes toward Isabella and then back to Ramona, not sure if this was a conversation to be had in front of her.

"Trust me, she's not as innocent as she looks, but that's another conversation. Right now I just need you to be real with me."

"Okay," I agreed, bracing myself.

"Do you know who shot me?" she asked.

"Yes."

"Did your father know?"

"Yes."

"And he let her live?"

"That was for me. He had her and Keyz moments after it happened, and he probably would've killed them both if not for what I was going through.

"You mean with the killing of the cop in California?"

"No, nothing ever came of that. I mean with Jordyn."

"What happened with her after I left?"

Again I looked over at my little sister, this time unwillingly to go on.

"Bella, I want you to go find your brother DJ for me, okay?"

"Yes, Mama."

"Wait. Deshana, do you have a gun on you?" Ramona asked.

I reached behind me and handled her my pistol. To my complete shock, she in turn gave it to Isabella.

"Do you know how to work it?" she asked.

Quickly and with precision, Bella dropped the clip and clearing the chamber before thumbing the bullet back into the clip, re-chambering the round, and flipping the safety on.

"What the fuck?" I murmured.

"Ok, go and find him, but don't shoot him," Ramona said.

"Of course not, Mama," she replied, laughing as she got out of the car.

"You're definitely gonna have to explain that," I told her, still not believing that a twelve-year-old was that cold with a gun.

"We'll get to that. Tell me what happened."

Without pride I told her about the way I'd butchered my little sister, and how I'd blacked out and blocked the episode from memory.

"When it was all said and done, I felt like I was getting ready to snap mentally, and I needed my dad. I knew I could've killed my grandmother, and he would've, but I needed him not to be the monster right then. Because if he would've killed her, the woman that gave him life, I would've only feared him from that point on, and I couldn't handle that. So, he banished her to New York to raise Devonte. I thought that was okay, but she raised him to hate his own father."

"I can see the guilt eating at you, Deshana. You know he wouldn't want that, you were his baby," she said, squeezing my hand. I knew there was some truth to her words, but still I couldn't let myself off the hook that easily.

"I love my daddy with all my heart, but this is my fault."

"Stop. I'll hear no more of that, you understand? I may not be able to walk, but I'll still kick your ass!"

"You-you can't walk?" I asked, horrified.

"Don't worry, it's only temporary. Shit, let's see you take a nap for over a decade and your legs not fall asleep!" she replied, laughing.

"So, how long will you stay?"

"Long enough to set things straight."

I didn't have to ask what she meant because the look in her eyes said it all. "Before you get off into that, you might wanna talk to DJ."

"Oh, that's definitely a must! Little DJ's been quite busy in my absence. Did he really start the war with his brother by kidnapping his pregnant girlfriend in the mall?"

"Oh yeah, but it's worse than that. That same pregnant girlfriend is now living in DJ's house with the baby, and DJ's fucking her," I informed her, hating the way the words tasted on my tongue.

"You're not serious."

"When it comes to thinking with his dick, he's just like our dad."

"But even he has to be smart enough to see the disaster in that decision! And what about the girl? She's got to be crazy for real."

"I don't know, but I will deal with her after the funeral. Speaking of which, there're still a million things to do, so come on, because you're helping."

"Damn, bossy ass!" she said, laughing.

I got out of the limo and helped her into the wheelchair one of her guards had waiting.

"Damn, their ears must be burning," I said spotting my grandmother and Brianna having a heated argument not far from the stage.

"That's her?" Ramona asked.

"Yeah. You know who she's talking to."

"Yep. They don't look happy with each other. Pity."

I laughed and pushed her into the house, and down the hall into my father's office.

"I liked the old house better," she said looking around.

"You can redecorate if you want."

"How you figure?"

"Because everything is yours in the event you woke up and dad was gone. He left you everything."

I could tell what I said surprised her, but it wasn't until we got to his office I saw she was crying.

"What's wrong?" I asked.

"He-he never stopped loving me," she sobbed.

"Of course not. Why would you think he would?"

"I don't know, I don't know."

I wrapped my arms around her and held her until the crying subsided a little. And then all hell broke loose.

"Do you hear that?" I asked.

"Yeah, it's a crowd of people, and it's getting louder."

"Stay here," I said, leaving the room at a dead run and heading for the foyer.

What I saw when I got there was just too ghetto for description. It was a crowd of muthafuckas in a circle like they were out front of a club, and in the middle two bitches were fighting hard. The light-skin one I didn't know, but she looked familiar. The other was one I hoped got her ass dragged.

Aryanna

Chapter Thirteen

Brianna

"DJ! DJ!"

"What, girl?"

"Come get this damn baby!" I screamed, beyond fed up with her non-stop crying.

I understood babies were supposed to cry, but there was absolutely nothing wrong with this little girl. Except that she wanted DJ.

"What's the matter with my baby, huh?" he said, taking her from my arms.

"She's spoiled rotten, and I wonder whose fault that is," I told him, disgusted at the fact she quieted right down for him.

"That's okay, pumpkin, your momma doesn't know what she's talking 'bout, does she? No, she doesn't. No, she doesn't," he said, baby talking her right into smiles and laughs.

"Like I said, spoiled. Come here so I can fix your tie."

After straightening his tie, I stepped back to admire how he looked in his suit. The occasion might be a sad one, but I couldn't deny how sexy the nigga looked in the all-black: Black Billionaires suit, black tie, white Gucci shirt and black Gucci loafers. With his dreads tied away from his face, I got to really see how handsome he was. And if anyone saw how he was playing with my daughter, they'd never imagine a gun in his hand.

"You look good," I said.

"I know. You don't look bad yourself," he replied, giving me a look that would get us in trouble.

"Behave," I warned, smoothing out my black, knee-length Gucci dress.

"I'm always well behaved. It be you that's with the bullshit. Matter of fact, come here."

Before I could stop him, he had me right up against him with his hand up my dress, his fingers gently caressing the soft silk of my boy shorts right where my clit was.

"DJ, don't! Don't start. There're way too many people outside, and you know we don't have enough time before the service."

"I'm just making sure you got underwear on. Now, if I was trying to start something, I'd do this."

Quick as a cat, he stuck his hand down inside my boy shorts and was using his middle finger to part my pussy lips in a 'come here' motion. Instantly I was wet and dripping all over his finger now moving inside me, causing my knees to rattle a little.

"Uh-uh, stop," I said, reluctantly stepping away, and ready to kick his ass for laughing at his effect on me. Then he had the nerve to lick his finger before giving me a quick kiss.

"We'll settle this later. I'ma take hope to CJ and then make sure everything is straight so we can get started," he said.

"Are you sure CJ is okay? I mean, it's gonna take more than a couple of days to get over what she saw."

"Yeah, it is, but she insists work is the best possible thing for her right now. Don't worry, if I didn't think she was up to it I wouldn't trust her with our baby."

"Our baby?" I asked, raising an eyebrow at his terminology.

He looked down at little Hope in his arms where she was all smiles trying to grab his hair, then he looked back at me.

"Yeah, our baby. You got a problem with that?"

I shook my head no, not trusting my voice because of what I'd seen. He looked at both of us with so much love, and it made my heart beat wildly. But I couldn't help wondering what Hope's father was doing at that exact moment, and if he was thinking about his daughter. I knew he probably hated me, and the truth was I still felt some type of way about him fucking Ruby, but none of that erased all the years we'd had together. Or the beautiful little girl we'd created.

"Is there anything you need me to do?" I asked.

"No, baby, you're fine," he replied with a wink as he left the bedroom.

Slipping on my black Gucci sneakers, I headed downstairs and out into the sea of faces who'd come to pay tribute. It was hard to believe a man so hated and so feared could have so many friends, but from what I'd come to know, nobody really knew Devaughn Mitchell. No matter how many people I asked, every one of them would probably give me a different answer or tell me a different story.

I got to see a kinder, gentler side of him, but I had no illusions about what he could become. His kids were like him in so many ways it was hard not to believe he was ruthless. Yet, as I walked past the local news crews, I knew they were here in part because of how generous he was when it came to giving back.

A lot of people can cut a check, and they'll never know where the money goes, nor do they care because it's a tax write-off. But from what I'd learned, Devaughn Mitchell gave what was needed. If a school needed computers, then he'd go to Best Buy and get them, and then deliver them personally. If a community needed a playground, then he'd go get a construction team and have them break ground in front of him and monitor it on a day-to-day basis. I saw a lot of him in DJ despite how hard he had to act at times, and that's why I considered him a good man. My good man.

"We need to talk," she said, taking my arm and pulling me next to the stage.

"Ms. Gladys, are you crazy? What are you doing here?" I demanded.

"In case you forgot, Devaughn was my son. Why shouldn't I be here?"

"Seriously? After what happened in the hospital with Deshana?"

"Let's talk about the hospital, little girl, because you lied to my face!"

"Huh? What are you talking about?" I asked with as much righteous indignation as I could manage, but I already knew.

"You know damn well what I'm talking about! You said Tae shot my son, but it wasn't Tae. It was DJ who pulled the trigger."

Deep down I knew that lie could only last so long, but it had still been a necessary lie. The question now was how was I gonna get her to keep her mouth shut.

"Ok, first of all, I told you I didn't know who shot Devaughn, and when Deshana asked there was a very large gun present. What was I supposed to say?"

"How about the truth, Brianna!"

"So, let me get this straight, you wanted me to tell Deshana her favorite little brother killed her father, when I'm not even sure that's what happened? Did you want her to kill DJ?"

"Oh, cut the shit, you know who shot my son! And I don't want anyone else to die, but why put it on Tae?"

"Tae's dead! Or at least everyone thinks he is. Who hunts down a dead man?"

"It's awfully convenient he's dead, too. Now you're here all cozy in the lap of fucking luxury while your fiancé can't even see his goddamn daughter!"

"Which one? He may have more than one child. I mean, if he got Ruby pregnant, lord knows who else he was fucking!"

"Ruby? Ruby was pregnant? How did you know that, because he never told me?"

"Listen, Ms. Gladys, I loved Tae — love Tae — but he's not the man I thought he was. He slaughtered innocent children, he cheated on me, and who knows what else he did."

"Tae would never do that, don't listen to their lies!"

I just gave her a sad smile because I knew how she felt.

"Yeah, I thought I knew him, too."

I turned to walk away from her, but she grabbed my arm again.

"At least tell me about the baby," she pleaded.

"Her name is Hope Amazing Briggs. She's happy and healthy."

"When can we see her?"

"I'll send you pictures of her tonight, but no face-to-face until things calm down around here."

"I hope you know what you're doing, Brianna."

"So do I," I mumbled, walking away.

I had a lot of love for Ms. Gladys, and I hoped she was smart enough to either leave or get somewhere and blend in. she was walking around in the open like she didn't know this family was the wrong kind of crazy.

I was moving without destination until I saw DJ headed toward the main house, and there was some light-skin chick following him. I felt a tug on my memory that quickened my stride, because this was the same female that had been in his house the day he'd brought me there. A lot had changed since then, and I had a feeling home girl would need to hear it from me.

"I appreciate you coming, and we will talk, but it'll have to be after."

"What up, baby?" I asked, interrupting him as I looped my arm through his. I felt the heat of her stare like she was Superwoman or some shit, but I gave her my best *bitch, please* smile.

"Um, excuse us, we're talking. Ain't you that bitch?"

"That's right, I am that bitch," I said, catching her flush with a right jab to the mouth, but only grazing her forehead with my left hook.

She backed up and squared up with me, and I liked that because I wasn't no hair-pulling type fighter. I was about that action. She fired a jab of her own that left the fresh taste of blood in my mouth, but I knew she felt my left-right combo when I switched from southpaw to orthodox.

By now there was a crowd around us and we were circling like two fighters in the ring. A missed right-cross got her stung with an uppercut, but she side-stepped my own right at the last minute and gave me a shot to the temple that tested my knees a little. Suddenly there was a girl standing in between us, about an inch or two shorter than me, holding her hands up for us to stop. It took a second for me to realize it was DJ's sister, Bella.

"Bella, move!" I ordered.

The other bitch saw this as her moment since I was distracted, but before I could react to her charge, Bella had her on her back.

"Today is my father's funeral. Enough!" she yelled, and with a quickness the crowd disappeared back out the door.

It was only then that I noticed Deshana standing there with a smile on her face.

"All of you, this way. Now," she said, turning and heading down a hallway.

I waited for the other bitch to get off the floor to see if she still had something on her mind, but the look DJ gave me forced me to walk in front of him and behind Bella. She led the way into an office where Deshana was sitting behind a desk and a woman in a wheelchair was sitting next to her.

I didn't know who the woman was, but she was gorgeous in a Dolce and Gabbana black dress with her long, curly hair pulled into a ponytail at the nape of her neck.

"Holy shit!" I heard DJ whisper from behind me.

"You're all grown up, huh, DJ?" the woman said, her voice hitching slightly.

"Mama? But it-it can't be," he replied softly.

"Did you miss me?"

He spoke no more words, but simply went to her, fell to his knees, put his head in her lap and wept. I'd never heard a man cry like that, so much sorrow and pain I feared he might drown in it. I hurt for him, and looking around, I didn't see one dry eye in the room. Finally he was able to get himself together enough to pull back and look up at the still-silently crying woman.

"You're really here?"

"I am. Now tell me, sweetheart, what have you done?"

For a moment I was struck with terror and the horrifying feeling he was gonna tell her everything, but he simply shook his head and put it back in her lap.

"DJ, listen to me. This is not what your mother would've wanted for you. I knew your mother. I loved your mother, and I know how differently she wanted your life to be, sweetheart."

"But, Mona, I had to, for her sake. I couldn't just let her die and it go unanswered like it meant nothing."

She nodded her head knowingly and continued to rub his head in her lap.

"Why were you two fighting?" Deshana asked me. Before I could say a word, that bitch was bumping her gums.

"I was talking to DJ when this bitch—"

I was moving toward her, ready to go on that ass again until Bella stepped in.

"I already told you once, and there won't be a second warning," she said, looking from one of us to the other.

"Little girl."

"I'd listen to her if I were you," Deshana warned me with a smile that didn't quiet reach her eyes.

"Whatever. I remembered this chick and I didn't appreciate the way she was all up on my dude."

"Your dude?" Ramona asked, popping DJ in the back of the head.

"Hold up, ain't you the one he kidnapped and you had a baby on his couch? His brother's baby?" the light-skinned girl asked with attitude.

I guess when she laid the facts out like that, it did sound bad, but she didn't have no reason to be in my business.

"And?" I said.

"Girl, phew! You've known him for, like, thirty seconds, and you sound real thirsty trying to claim your baby's daddy's brother.

"Who's thirsty, ho, when you the one showing up uninvited, wearing a fucking sundress to a funeral. Looks like you shopping for a man, boo boo."

"Nah, I just didn't have nothing else that fit."

"Why you making your problems our problems, fat ass?"

"Oh, it ain't your problem, me and DJ can handle it," she replied, smiling.

"Trust me, my man is more than happy with what he has now," I told her, smirking.

"You two, enough!" DJ said, getting to his feet and walking over to us. "Brianna, chill. And CoCo, did you come here to start drama on today of all days?"

"No, I just came to console my baby daddy."

"Huh?" he said weakly.

I knew what was coming, but I prayed she wouldn't say it.

"You heard me, DJ. I'm pregnant."

Before he could respond, the sound of gunfire ripped through the air. Somebody brought death to a funeral.

Aryanna

Chapter Fourteen

DJ

I turned the T.V. off, tired of hearing the same news report on every station talking about the mayhem at my father's funeral. It wasn't like I hadn't been there when the shit started.

"Tell me what happened," I said, slowly passing around my living room.

"DJ, we've been over this."

"I'm not talking to you, Brianna; I'm talking to my sister. DayDay, tell me again what happened."

When she looked at me, I could see the pain and anger in her eyes, but I didn't mind because it was a welcome change from the vacancy signs that had been there for days.

"Ready and I had just finished smoking a blunt, and we were getting off the bus to rehearse for our performance. I was coming down the stairs when I saw him, but I didn't pay attention at first because he was just standing there next to his car. When he came onto the property, he looked my way, and that's when I knew."

"Knew what?" I prodded.

"Knew who he was."

"And how did you know?" Deshana asked.

"I told you, it was his eyes. His eyes reminded me of Dad's and DJ's."

"And then?" I asked.

"I don't know. I just pulled my gun and started shooting. I snapped because he'd have the nerve to actually be here today, of all days."

"Did he shoot back or reach for a gun?" Deshana asked.

"No, he dove for the car. Once he got in, they pulled off."

"Ready?" I asked.

"Homie, all I saw was the car hauling ass away from us and DayDay shooting at it. Everything happened so fast, and I was so damn high."

"And why did you think it was a good idea for you and my sister to get high right before our father's funeral?" I asked, fixing him with a look of disgust.

"That was my idea, DJ," Deshana said. I turned a quizzical glance in her direction.

"When Ready came to holla at me about DayDay, I didn't have time to check on her, and I figured it was just her upset and nervous. So, I told him to get her high and rehearse, but what the fuck did you put in the blunt, li'l homie?"

"All I had on me was some K2, and it doesn't last as long as that loud would, anyway," he replied, defensive.

Being that the world of synthetic drugs had become my playground, I knew all about synthetic marijuana. Some of that shit was mild, so it kinda simulated a weed high, but some of it would have you high out your mind to the point you didn't know what planet you were on. Literally.

"So, you smoked a blunt of K2, and now you want me to believe you saw a dead man?" I asked very slowly.

"You can believe what you want, but I'm telling you I saw Devonte at our father's funeral today, and that's why I started shooting. Do you think I'd just do some shit like that for laughs?"

"I didn't think you knew how to shoot a gun, period, let alone when to shoot the muthafucka! And I think you were high out of your goddamn biscuit and so fucked up about what happened to Dad that you don't know what you saw."

"Well, check the cameras, smartass! Don't act like this muthafucka ain't wired up tighter than a bank!" she yelled in frustration.

"We did that first, sweetheart, but your bus was blocking our view," Deshana said, trying to soothe Sharday.

"Just great. You know what, believe whatever the fuck you wanna believe. Ms. Lynch, what am I looking at legally?"

"Well, no one saw you shooting, so the cops really have more questions than answers. Fortunately for you, all the questions and attention is focused on your brother at this moment," Victoria replied.

"It's okay, he can handle it, right DJ? I mean, you are your father's son. Deshana, I love you, but I'm going back on tour," she said, getting up and leaving the living room without a backward glance.

"Stay with her, Ready Roc, and don't let shit happen," Deshana ordered.

"You got it, homie."

"Wait. What did she say the girl looked like, Ready?" I asked.

"She said it was a white girl, but she had glasses and a hat on."

I nodded my head as he followed DayDay out the door, but now my eyes were searching Brianna's face. She held my gaze and didn't flinch in the slightest, which meant she was an accomplished liar or she had nothing to worry about.

"Did you ever find out what happened to that girl Tae brought to the hospital?" I asked her.

"Yes, apparently she died from a shotgun blast to the side. Why?"

"Just curious. I mean, I know all about K2 and what it can do, but I've never known my big sister to flip out."

"Okay, so what are you really asking me, DJ?" she asked with a slight tilt of her head.

"There's no double meanings, sweetheart, my question was all I wanted to know. I do need to have a meeting, though, before everyone has to leave, so can you go spend some time with Hope?" I suggested.

The look on her face said she wanted to argue, but why would she? We both knew my business didn't concern her, and it never would.

"Everyone, let's go to my office," I said.

Once I had the door open, I ushered everyone inside before locking us in and taking a seat behind my desk.

"First things first, Deshana, let's deal with your end before we get into the family drama," I said

"Okay. As far as I know, you know most of the homies I've dealt with out here since coming back east, but this is one that represents the same hood I do. D.O.E is rolling sixty Crip out of Nola, and he's gonna handle shit for the entire south, meaning we'll ship everything to him and he'll get it to all the other hoods."

"Can you handle all that?" I asked him.

"If I couldn't, I wouldn't be here. I'm 'bout my money, and I don't let nothing stand in the way of that," he replied, looking at me intently. His eyes told stories of death, but not apology.

He had that dark complexion I would associate with a Haitian, but I could still see the sixty tatted under his eye that was a source of pride. The slight build didn't give any illusions of weakness, and I'd never known my sister to fuck with a lame nigga after that shit Kevin had pulled on our family.

"We're talking hundreds of millions of dollars," I said. This got a small smile from him.

"If we were talking about lunch money, I wouldn't be here," he replied.

"Let's do it, then," I said, extending my hand and shaking his.

I opened the door and told him to have a seat on the couch until my sister came out, then I resumed my position back behind my desk. It felt good to be in the presence of my team again, and I had a feeling I was gonna need them now more than ever.

Evy kept giving me knowing glances from underneath that mop of blonde hair on his head, and I knew it was because he really didn't like being around people. Victoria was silently evaluating everyone in the room, sizing them up like she would in a courtroom, but that's what made her such a good judge of character.

Brittany was the unruly wildcard in my group. She was 5'10", 170 pounds of tornado, and I never knew which way she was gonna blow. One minute she could be cool, calm, and collected, like she was right now, but in the blink of an eye she'd be so angry you'd ask yourself what fresh hell this was. Maybe it was the red hair that made her crazy.

I had inherited a weakness for white women that I'd thoroughly explored while at school, but redheads made me nervous. Harley had been Brittany's balance, but now, with her gone, I didn't know what to expect.

"I really appreciate you all coming out here for me," I said, looking at them one by one.

"Tell us what we're doing, DJ," Brittany said, sitting on my desk next to me.

"First, I need to introduce you all to someone very important to me. I know you're wondering because she hasn't said much, but this is Ramona Mitchell, my dad's wife."

"Wait, you mean *the* Ramona?" Evy asked, looking from me to her.

"What does that mean, *the* Ramona?" Ramona asked, smiling.

"It's just. I didn't mean any disrespect!"

"He's my computer wizard, so of course before he came to work for me he would've done his homework."

"Ah, so he works for you, DJ? And what does that work consist of?"

I felt like the conversation was getting ready to go left, because I knew she wouldn't approve of what I was doing. Reminding her I was grown would probably get the shit slapped out of me.

"A little of this and that, but we call him Mad Hacker for a reason," I replied.

"I see," she said, giving me a look I didn't entirely understand. Deshana putting a hand on her shoulder, stopped whatever she'd been about to say.

"To answer your question, Britt, we're gonna do what we've been doing, as in making money, but on a bigger scale. With my father being gone, there're gonna be a lot of people who want to take his spot, and we can't allow that. As far as the muscle goes, my sister Deshana and her wife JuJu rule with iron fists, so all we have to worry about is manufacturing and keeping our money clean."

"What about the murder charge you're facing?" Brittany asked.

"I got that covered," Victoria said.

"Don't worry, I won't be going to jail anytime soon, and even if I do get indicted, you know what to do next."

"You mean Plan B?" Brittany asked, somewhat nervously.

"Of course, why?"

"DJ, are you sure about that? I mean, I feel like you're not trusting my skills and connections," Victoria said.

"What's Plan B?" Ramona asked.

At first I just looked at her, because I really didn't wanna give her an answer, but the look she was giving me told me she wasn't gonna take being ignored or bullshitted.

"Plan B is just the necessary steps that have to be taken to get me out if they locked me up," I replied.

"And what are those steps?" she asked, insistently.

"Well, first they would find out who the judge and prosecutor are, then the prosecutor would be snatched so the judge got the message that coming after me ain't worth the fallout."

Surprisingly, her immediate response was to laugh out loud, but her expression quickly became deadly serious.

"So, let me get this straight: you're plans involve kidnapping and possibly murdering government officials?"

"Yeah," I replied, feeling a little self-conscious under her intense gaze.

She stared at me for what felt like an eternity, and then she wheeled herself over to my office door and opened it.

"Everybody get out," she ordered.

"Excuse me?" Brittany replied.

"You heard her," Deshana said, getting up.

Brittany was smart enough not to say another word, and one-by-one everyone followed her lead out of my office until we were alone. Even with my big-ass desk between us, I still felt smothered by her presence. My childhood memories of Ramona were of a beautiful, kind woman that treated me like her own son, but as I'd gotten older I'd learned more about who she was and who she was connected to. That didn't change my love for her, but it did bring some needed caution into the equation.

"DJ, what are you doing?"

"What do you mean?"

"You know damn well what I mean! There's no way your father would've approved of you being a fucking drug dealer, so where did you get the idea that it's okay to be Pablo Escobar all of a sudden?"

"It's not all of a sudden, and dad knew before he died. He sent me away to school to find my way."

"He sent you away to school to get an education and make something better of your life!" she yelled, pushing her wheelchair right in front of my desk.

"And I have. I'm not some corner drug dealer hustling for sneaker money."

"Is that what it's about, the money? Sweetheart, we've got more money than your grandchildren can spend in their lifetime, and it grows legally every day."

"I know that, but it's also about my legacy."

"DJ, just because you're named after your father doesn't mean you have to be like him. He was lucky, but you're fortunate. Your legacy can be greater than his if you do it the right way."

The love in her eyes told me she still cared, but I could see she didn't understand. I understood what was inside me, but I couldn't put it into words. I loved my father, despite all that had happened, but if there was one thing I learned from him it was great men never lived in the shadows of others.

"Ramona, I'm not concerned with doing it the right way. I just have to do it my way," I said patiently.

"That's some of the dumbest shit I've ever heard! You're setting yourself up for failure, DJ. Think about it. Kidnapping government officials, fucking your brother's baby mama. I mean, does any of that sound smart to you?"

"One has nothing to do with the other, and in either case I know what I'm doing."

Her response was a somewhat dismissive snort that pissed me off, but I held my tongue.

"I don't understand how you grew up at your father's feet and yet still don't know how to play chess."

"I know how to play chess."

"Moving pieces ain't playing chess, especially if you can't even see the board," she replied condescendingly.

"Like I said before, I know what I'm doing, and I'm old enough to make these decisions now without anyone's approval."

"You're right, but how long do you think it'll be before it all comes crashing down on your head? You're getting ready to be a father, DJ, not to mention the baby you're already raising with the ho upstairs. How does all that fit into the equation?"

I wanted to admit this was a good question I hadn't had a chance to wrap my mind around, but I wouldn't give her the satisfaction.

"I got this," replied stubbornly.

"Okay, we'll see. I'm gonna make it a little easier on you, though. I know your dad left everything to me, so I'll handle all the businesses and make sure things are in order."

"But."

"Don't worry, I'm not cutting you out of anything, but I will make damn sure everything your father worked for doesn't burn to the ground because of your bullshit. You can either accept that or do it all on your own."

It was on the tip of my tongue to recommend a beach in hell, but that seemed counter-productive.

"Fine," I said through gritted teeth.

"Good. The first thing I need you to do is get your personal life together."

"What do you mean?"

"I mean your shit is messier than an old Love and Hip Hop episode. If you didn't learn shit else from your father, you should've learned the consequences for thinking with your dick."

"I got it under control."

"Really? Okay, well, there are three women in this house right now, and I'll bet you a quarter of a billion you've fucked them all."

I opened my mouth to reply, but the smirk she was giving me reduced me to laughter instead.

"Just like I thought. Listen, I'm going back to New York for a while to tie up some loose ends, and by the time I get back I want you to have your shit together, understood?"

"Yes, Mona."

"Good. Now, come give me a kiss and push me to my car."

I did as she requested, loving the feeling of being wrapped in her arms even though I'd been scolded. Ramona was the closest thing I had to a mother, and she was all I had left. I knew what she said to me was only because she loved me, and she would do anything to protect me, even if that meant protecting me from myself.

After sending her off, I came back into the house to tell everyone we could resume our meeting tomorrow and showed them to their rooms. I knew a conversation was needed between Courtney and I, but when I got to her room she was sleeping peacefully.

I didn't know how to feel about her anymore. I loved knowing she was gonna have my baby because I knew she'd be a great mom and cherish that child always. At the same time, I couldn't help wishing she was someone else. When I finally walked into my own bedroom, I found Brianna lying in bed completely naked with the dome open, allowing the moonlight and stars to add an almost spiritual glow to her gorgeous body.

Immediately my mouth began to water, and suddenly my suit was entirely too hot to have on any longer. I drank her beauty in with my eyes as I moved toward her, undressing along the way. By the time I'd reached the bed, all I was wearing were my socks and a smile.

"I've been waiting for you," she whispered to me.

"I see that."

"We need to talk."

"Seriously? Right now?"

"Mm-hmm," she replied, motioning for me to get in bed beside her.

I did as she asked, pulling her toward me until we were eye-to-eye and only a breath away.

"What is it, babe?"

"I-I love you, DJ."

"I know," I replied, smiling.

"I don't know how we got to this point, but there's no turning back for me. That scares me."

"Baby, you don't have to be scared. You know I love you, too."

"I know that, and I feel that, but now you're expecting a child with another woman."

"Shh," I said, pressing my finger to her lips before she could start rambling. "That changes nothing. All you have to say is that you're down to have another baby, because there's nothing I won't give you."

"What if I want more than that?" she asked softly.

"What is it you want, Bri?"

She didn't respond with words first, but simply rolled on top of me and took me inside her so quickly I forgot to breathe for a second. Slowly she began to move up and down, rising high enough to only have the head of my dick inside her before taking all of me again. The beauty of the moonlight and shadows dancing across her face left me speechless, but the tears in her eyes spoke volumes to me.

"I want. I want you," she said huskily.

"You've got me, babe."

"All of you."

"Yes, Bri, yes."

"Promise?"

"I do."

"Then marry me."

Chapter Fifteen

Devonte

Six Months Later

"Thought I'd find you out here," Amber said, sitting beside me on the back porch.

"Yeah, I'm just out here thinking," I replied.

"What's on your mind?"

"Everything. I don't know why, but somehow when I come out here and stare at all these damn trees it helps organize my thoughts."

"Let me find out you're a country muthafucka at heart!" she said, laughing.

"I wouldn't go that far, but I will say that in these last six months, I've found a peace that don't exist in city life."

"Yeah, I know what you mean. I think being near death and losing so much has made us look at the world differently."

I contemplated that statement for a moment and realized how true it was. I'd grown up in a different world, surrounded by things that seemed more important than what they really were. Being in hiding for half a year made me see shit differently, but it also made me realize what was important. What was worth dying for.

"You know I couldn't have done this without you, right?" I asked, turning toward her.

"I know. But I couldn't have done it without you, either. The gunshot wound would've healed eventually, but I don't know about my heart."

"I know what you mean, and I love you, too."

"I didn't say all that, now," she said, laughing.

"Whatever, Ma, you know you do," I teased, pushing her lightly.

"Yeah, yeah. Are you gonna tell me what's really on your mind now, because I know it ain't how much you love me. My pussy is good, but it ain't gonna have you out here looking at no damn trees for hours."

I laughed at that and started to tell her just how good her pussy was, but I knew she'd see I was avoiding the bigger question.

"My baby girl is almost eight months old, and I haven't seen more than a few pictures of her. I haven't gotten to hold her or smell her little baby smell. I haven't gotten to hear her little baby gibberish or try to teach her to say daddy. I mean, it's been six months since my father's funeral. How fucking long am I expected to wait?"

"I know it's hard, Tae, even though I can't imagine how you're feeling. The reality is we fucked up six months ago by going to the funeral."

"I was just trying to protect my grandmother."

"I know that, but still, you were spotted."

"What was I supposed to do? Listen to the woman I loved talk about me like she didn't give a damn, and then find out I hadn't just lost my best friend, but another child as well?"

"Like I said, I can't imagine what you're feeling. At the same time, you know we weren't ready to go up against your brother and his family."

"That was then," I replied, looking at her.

"Ah, so that's what's on your mind. You're ready to go after him?"

I let my silence speak for me as I slowly rotated my arm first clockwise, then counter clockwise. Six months of working out with Tiffany had not only repaired the damage from my gunshot wounds, but it had me in better shape than I could ever remember being.

Physically I was ready for war, but mentally I was set on absolute destruction.

"What's the plan?"

"I don't know yet. I'm still thinking."

"Well, think out loud and let me in, goddamn it!" she said in frustration.

"Okay. I want to take from him everything he loves. And only then will I take his life."

"I like the sound of that, so where would we start?"

"How much did Josh teach you about hacking?"

"I'm not as good as him, but I still know my way through cyber space."

"Okay, well, the first thing we gotta do is find out what this nigga has been doing and who he's doing it with."

"Then what?"

"Then we're gonna send all of his associates video footage of him meeting with the FBI, DEA, and ATF, which will definitely make his friends his enemies."

"Where are we getting this video from?"

"We're gonna make it," I replied, smiling.

"Huh?"

"You heard me. Him and I do favor each other."

"Ah, so that's why you grew those ugly-ass dreads!" she said, tugging on one and smiling.

"I just figured since he thinks he's that nigga, then he can do this with the bare essentials like we are."

"I like how you think, but this is gonna take a lot of work."

"It's worth it, though," I said, pulling her toward me and kissing her lips gently.

"Tae, you're distracting me," she said in between our kisses.

"Sorry. Go grab the laptop so we can get to work."

After biting my lip and sucking on it a little, she got up to go back into the house, once again leaving me with my thoughts. This idea I had of turning everyone against DJ had come to me suddenly one day, but the more I'd thought on it, the more it made sense.

One thing I'd learned in that wolf pack known as the Bloods was everything was based on what a person thought they knew. A homie was only a homie as long as he was viewed as a standup guy, but anything less would have him killed, and his friends, too, if they didn't distant themselves from him. It was my belief that all criminal organizations thought the same, so if we did this right, then at the very least he'd be left out in the cold.

I heard the door open behind me and Tiffany, Maurice, my grandmother, and Amber filed out, everyone taking a seat and looking in my direction.

"What?" I asked self-consciously.

"Amber said you needed to talk to us," my grandmother replied, looking at me and then her.

"Lay it out for them, Tae," Amber said.

I proceeded to run the first part of my plan down to them, watching their expressions for any sign of confusion or disapproval.

"Once you send the video, what's your next move?" Maurice asked.

"Well, even if all his outside help abandons him, he still has our sister Deshana, so I was thinking it's time she got that recording we made at our father's funeral."

"But she doesn't say DJ shot Devaughn," my grandmother reminded me.

"You're right, but it does say Tae is still alive, and Brianna knew about it," Amber interjected.

"Which will automatically cause problems in that household, and it should make DJ sweat a little more because he'll know it's only a certain amount of time before it comes out that he shot his father," Tiffany said.

"He'll kill Brianna," my grandmother said, looking at me closely.

"That ain't my problem."

"Tae."

"Grandma, what do you want me to say? She chose her path! I understand her saying she wanted peace, but how does that translate into her playing house with that nigga? With my daughter!"

"Your actions pushed her away! You may not have shot any of those kids yourself, and you may not have started this war, but what did you do to stop it? Brianna may have thought she knew what your life was about, but she didn't, so can you blame her for being scared when she realized the boogie man was real?"

"So, I'm the boogie man? That nigga kidnapped her while she was pregnant!" I yelled, jumping to my feet.

"The bottom line is we don't know how she came to love your brother, but she's still your daughter's mother," Tiffany said, stepping in between me and my grandmother.

"My only concern is Hope," I replied.

"How do you plan to keep her safe and get her back if her mom's dead?" my grandmother asked.

Leave it to her to find the one question I didn't have a ready answer for. I couldn't let anything happen to my baby girl. I wouldn't be able to live with myself if she was hurt because of me.

"What if we went in and got her before he sent the tape of Brianna?" Amber asked, opening up the laptop in front of her.

"How?" Tiffany asked.

"Well, if I remember correctly, it wasn't exactly Fort Knox, which means we can get onto the property," Amber replied.

"Yeah, but going onto his turf puts us out-manned and out-gunned," I replied, shaking my head.

"I think it'll be easier to simply have Brianna come to us," my grandmother said.

We all looked at her expectantly, waiting to hear her plan to make the impossible happen.

"If we show Brianna DJ is soon to be a walking dead man, her survival instincts will make her remove her and Hope from that situation."

Everyone let that simple logic roll around in their minds until, one-by-one, we were all shaking our heads in agreement.

"That's check, slim. The trick is to make the next move checkmate," Maurice advised.

"I agree. What I need from you all is some white people and a meeting place so we can make our video," I said.

"Let me and my wife make some calls and put some shit together. Ms. Gladys, why don't you reach out to Bri and see if she'll meet you in a neutral spot."

"Okay," she agreed.

The three of them went back into the house, leaving me and Amber to gather information. We spent the remaining daylight hours and on into the night learning all we could about the "Whiz Kid" and his activities. From the looks of things, our father's shoes fit him well, but he was more ambitious, which made him less particular about who he got in bed with.

From the Crips to the Columbians, and all the way up to the Yakuza, DJ was supplying the masses with his dope. The biggest surprise we found came from the fact my father's first wife had somehow come out of her thirteen-year coma. I hadn't seen her in that long, but her face was burned into my mind the way my aunt Victoria's face had been since the moment she was killed in front of me.

Despite the fact Ramona had returned me unharmed physically, what she'd done to me mentally had to be answered for. Keeping my emotions in check, I understood taking them both out at once was asking for death, so I would have to exercise patience. I couldn't put into words how tired I was of being patient, but still, when I climbed into bed in search of sleep, I felt the beginnings of some of my restlessness start to leave. It felt good to take action.

We spent the next seventy-two hours under the gun like we were working on Steven Spielberg project, but everyone understood the video had to be perfect or it wouldn't work. It worked in our favor to find out DJ had somehow maneuvered around a murder conviction, because it lent credibility to the fact shit wasn't right. We were gonna sell a dream, and everyone would buy it without question.

"How long is the video?" my grandmother asked, coming into the kitchen where Amber and I sat huddled over the laptop.

"It's only a few minutes long, like it's the initial meeting where they discuss what his cooperation will consist of," Amber replied.

"Is that enough?"

"Oh, hell yeah! Even a suspicion of being a snitch will get you fucked off in this game," I said.

"You can't release it yet, though."

"Why?" I asked, looking up at my grandmother.

"Because I still ain't heard back from Brianna."

This did pose a problem for all the reasons stated days ago, but I'd expected her to be in touch with her by now. I didn't know what to make of her silence, and honestly it was hard for me to care.

"Amber, I want you to send a copy of the video to her, and Grandma, you send her the audio from your conversation with her. She's got twenty-four hours to respond."

"And then what?" my grandmother asked.
"And then she is a casualty of this war."

Chapter Sixteen

Deshana

"Baby. Baby, wake up."

"Hm?"

"Deshana?"

"Yes, baby?" I answered, reluctantly pulling the comforter from over my head.

I had to blink my eyes a couple times to make sure I wasn't seeing shit, but the sight in front of me cleared my mind quickly. JuJu was standing next to the bed on her side, holding a tray with a huge plate of food on it. The aroma of sausage, fried potatoes, eggs, and bacon punching me in the nose. The smells alone had my stomach growling, but that was secondary to the throbbing beginning between my legs.

She sat the tray on the bed next to me so I could get a good look at her gorgeous naked body, and look I did. From her hard nipples that were calling to me like licorice bites, on down to the triangle she had shaved in a "D" that covered her treasures, I looked. I don't know when the music started, but I could hear The Deele singing their 1988 hit *I Only Think of You on Two Occasions*, and my mouth began to water a my beautiful wife swayed to the beat. I wanted to reach out to her, but I was transfixed by the seductive dance she was giving me.

"Come here, babe," I whispered huskily.

"Patience, sweetheart, I'm not going anywhere. Today is all about us," she replied, slowly climbing into the bed until there was only the plate of food between us.

"Sit up," she ordered.

I did what she said dutifully and allowed her to feed me breakfast in bed. We had money, power, and respect, but it was the little things like this that mattered more than anything to us.

The Deele's musical stylistics gave way to the legendary Patti Labelle singing *If Only You Knew*, and my love for this woman became so overwhelming that not another moment could be wasted eating breakfast.

"Put the food away," I ordered, lying back down on the bed.

Once she had everything out of our way, I pulled her to me, kissing her soft, plump lips with all the passion she ignited in me.

"Happy anniversary, baby," she murmured into my mouth.

"Happy anniversary to you, my wife," I replied, pausing only long enough to pull the t-shirt I'd been sleeping in over my head.

"Now, I'm still hungry, so sit on my face. And don't think about getting up until I've had enough."

She laughed, but did exactly as I demanded. The first taste of her was comparable to nothing, and no matter how many times we did this, it was always a brand new adventure. Her pussy talked to me, and I talked back, sucking on her clit until the floodgates opened and her delicious juices tsunamied into my mouth. I ate and drank her greedily, cupping her soft ass with force so she couldn't run until I'd had my fill.

"Baby! Baby, please! I c-can't cum again!" she whispered.

Pulling her toward me slightly, I stuck my tongue deep inside her tight asshole and proceeded to work her thoroughly, intent on proving her wrong.

"Oh! My! God!" she screamed as another orgasm rocketed through her body.

I knew she couldn't see me smiling beneath her, but I knew she felt it.

"Please, babe! Oh God, please!" she begged.

Digging my nails into her ass, I forced her to ride my face while I played Double Dutch with her pussy and ass. When she climaxed again, I finally let her collapse on the bed next to me, my smile one of complete satisfaction.

"K-keep smiling, because it's my turn next," she warned.

"You're threatening me with a good time, sweetheart."

"We'll see. Who the fuck keeps calling this early in the morning?"

It wasn't until she pointed it out that I realized the phone had been ringing for a while. Between the music playing and the tunnel vision I had for the beautiful woman lying next to me, I had tuned everything else out. It wasn't just the house phone ringing, though; our cellphones were going off, too. I reached for my phone only to feel myself being pulled back.

"Uh-uh, whatever it is can wait until later. This is our time right now," she said, getting on top of me, her fingers already working inside my tight pussy.

Suddenly the ringing was replaced by a buzzing in my ears as her lips worked in rhythm to her fingers, kissing with purpose all over my body.

"Whatever you say baby," I sighed as her teeth grazed my nipple before she began sucking.

Even with my eyes closed I could see colors on the back of my eyelids, and when I felt her tongue slip in between my pussy lips, those colors exploded, causing me to grab her by the hair.

"Hell yeah, do that sh—"

The sound of pounding on the penthouse door snapped me out of my zone and caused us both to freeze. All our phones were ringing, and someone was pounding on our door. Whatever was going on had to be damn important.

"You answer the phone and I'll get the door," I said, hopping up and grabbing my t-shirt, shorts, and pistol.

"Who is it?" I hollered, still a few feet from the door in case someone wanted to shoot first.

"Building security, Mrs. Mitchell," came the reply.

"Password?" I asked, chambering a round into my Glock .19.

"Oh, love," he said.

When I'd taken over LaLa's penthouse and the building, I'd implemented my own security team and turned our spot into a fortress. I didn't think the day would come when I'd have to lock the muthafucka down, but obviously something wasn't right.

I opened the door to find three heavily-armed men standing in front of me, one facing me while the other two watched for any signs of danger.

"What is it?"

"Ma'am, we received a call from one of the homies that said you might be in trouble, and to check on you immediately because you weren't answering your phone."

"We're fine, and what homie called you?"

"Ready Roc, ma'am."

"Okay, I'll call him. Has there been anything out of the ordinary happening this morning?"

"No, ma'am."

"Keep your eyes open from the ground to the roof, got it?"

"Yes, ma'am."

I closed the door to find JuJu standing in the middle of the living room with a look of uncertainty on her face.

"Was that Ready on the phone?" I asked.

"No, it-it was Ill Will."

"Ill Will? As in?"

"Yeah."

Ill Will was one of the big homies running Grape Street Crips out on the west coast. Grape Street was an original hood out of Jordan Downs Projects, and for that reason we paid homage to all it stood for. Even though Ill Will was originally from Memphis, TN, he'd relocated out west to take over when his big homie passed away, but I hadn't heard from him directly in years. Him calling out of the blue was unsettling.

"What did he say?" I asked, walking toward her.

"He said you've been summoned to a meeting out west. Immediately.

"Summoned? By who?"

"By all the big homies for the hoods we're aligned with."

To my knowledge there wasn't a meeting this month, so the gathering of the council must have been a last minute decision. That meant something was going on, and it was something major.

"A'ight, call and get the plane ready while I call Ready Roc," I told her.

"Ready Roc? Why?"

"I don't know. He called down here and told security to check on us, which he wouldn't do without a damn good reason."

"True. Well, I'll get the travel plans ready and get us packed to leave."

We both went back into our bedroom and got to work. Ready's phone rang once before he answered.

"What's crackin', homie?" I asked.

"Damn, why you ain't been answering your phone?" he asked, both relief and irritation lacing his voice.

"I was busy, and remember who you talking to, li'l homie."

"No disrespect intended, but I thought you'd wanna know someone shot at your sister's tour bus."

"They did what? She's okay, though, right? I mean, that muthafucka is bulletproof."

"Bulletproof, yes, but we got hit with a fucking rocket launcher, my nigga! We're fine, but it was some private shit, for real!"

"Start from the beginning," I ordered, sitting on the edge of my bed before my knocking knees forced me to the floor.

"We were finishing up a show in Texas and heading home when five black SUVs ran down on us, shooting and shit. The bullets bounced off, and so we just kept pushing, but once that rocket hit the back of the bus we were forced to pull over. Luckily we were deep, and you know I keep a war chest on board, so we got it crackin' with them muthafuckas."

"What did they look like?"

"It was dark, but they were Spanish for sure."

My mind started running through options, and even though it made absolutely no sense, I could only come to one conclusion.

"That's the Mexican mafia territory, but we don't have any beef with them," I said.

"That's what I thought, too."

"Okay, but even if we did, why would they go after Sharday? Everybody knows she is neutral."

"I don't know, big homie. We didn't have any problems in Texas, and we put on a good show. I was calling you to see if anything changed that I needed to know about."

"I don't know, either, but I'm on my way to a sit-down out west with the rest of the big homies, and maybe they'll have the answers. Where are you?"

"We're in Louisiana right now, headed for New Orleans."

"Okay, you'll be safe with D.O.E. I want you to call me as soon as you get there, understand?"

"I got you, big homie."

"And Ready, don't let shit happen to my sister."

"I won't," he replied before disconnecting.

"What happened?" JuJu asked.

I ran down to her what Ready told me as I scrambled to get dressed and get our shit together. I didn't have all the pieces to the puzzle, but it was evident a move was being made against us for whatever reason.

"The plane has to be refueled because your brother just got back from New York," JuJu informed me.

"New York? What the fuck was he doing in New York?" Asking her that question was pointless, and I had bigger problems than worrying about DJ right now. I did need to talk to him, though, but that could wait until I was on the plane.

"Call for the car," I told her.

"I'm on it. How heavy are we traveling?"

I knew she meant weapons, and ordinarily we'd just pick some shit up once we landed. But this didn't feel ordinary at all.

"I don't know what we're walking into, so let's be smart. Be ready for war, because something's up."

Aryanna

Chapter Seventeen

Brianna

"Come on, DJ, answer the phone!" I yelled in frustration at the constant ringing in my ear.

For the better part of twenty-four hours I'd been trying to get him on the phone, but it seemed my husband was too busy to be bothered. No matter how much I wished this was out of the ordinary, the truth was he'd become more and more busy over the last six months. I wasn't feeling neglected because he still gave Hope and me plenty of attention, but right then I was almost in a full panic because I couldn't get to him.

I had to explain before he saw the video and heard the recording. I had to make him see I'd only lied out of love, and because I wanted us to have a somewhat normal life together. But first I had to make sure he was okay. I hung up the phone while it was still ringing and dialed his number again, hoping for different results.

"Still no word from him?" CJ asked, walking into the living room.

"No. Where's Hope?"

"Down for her nap."

"Listen, you might have to leave here and take Hope somewhere safe."

"Somewhere safe? What's safer than this house? You're both completely protected."

"Casey, are you gonna argue with me, or are you gonna assure me I can trust my daughter with you?"

"Of course you can trust me, Brianna, but — but what about you? If you feel it's unsafe for Hope here, then why would you stay here?"

"Because he's my husband, and I can't leave his side. I owe him that much."

"But you're pregnant."

I needed no reminding of this. Still, my hand went to my stomach in a motion to protect my sleeping baby boy. I wanted him to be safe more than anything, but I wouldn't abandon his father when this was as much my fault as it was his. It was crazy how life worked, because it seemed like shit didn't go completely to hell until I was happy. Maybe I just didn't deserve happiness or a happily ever after. I couldn't stop wanting either, though, or I'd be accepting the worst kind of defeat.

"DJ will protect me, but we can't look after each other while we worry about our daughter, so I need you to take her."

"When?"

He still wasn't answering his phone, so I once again disconnected and thought about the simple, yet serious question she'd asked. The message I'd received had given me a day to bring myself and Hope to safety, but that was a day ago. Quickly I sent a text to Ms. Gladys and told her and her idiot grandson, before he got us all killed.

"I want you to take her now, CJ. Go get her stuff together, and I'll get you some traveling cash."

She headed up the stairs, and I went to DJ's office where his wall safe was located. After placing my palm on the scanner and unlocking the safe, I pulled out five hundred thousand dollars in cash and put it in a briefcase. I didn't expect to be away from my baby for that long, but it was better to be safe than sorry. With the money in hand, I went back into the living room and tried to call DJ again.

This time his phone went straight to voicemail, and the thought of what that might mean forced my heart down to my stomach. He wouldn't simply ignore my call. I called right back and got the same results, only now I could taste the panic on my tongue and feel the fear pounding in my temples.

"Think, Brianna, think!" I said aloud, wondering if I should call Deshana.

As quickly as that idea came to mind, I had to dismiss it, because when the truth was separated from the lies, she'd kill me. Pregnant or not.

"Okay, I've got what we'll need, and anything else we'll have to buy," CJ said, coming downstairs with Hope and a duffel bag in her arms.

Just looking at my baby girl, my firstborn, I didn't know how I could let her leave this house without me. It was my job to protect her, so how could I simply hand her over to a stranger? What were my options, though? Shit was about to hit the fan, and nobody would escape the fallout from it. In this moment, I had to love my daughter enough to let her go.

"Give her to me and put everything in the car," I said, holding the briefcase out and exchanging it for my sleepy-eyed little girl.

"Which car?"

"Don't take yours. Take the blue Porsche in case anyone thinks to come looking for you."

"Looking for me? Who would come looking for me?" she asked, alarmed.

I looked down at my beautiful Hope, who was already dozing back off against my chest. She looked so peaceful and innocent, and there was no way I could let anyone take that from her. Sooner than I'd like, the world would show her just how harsh it was, but not now, not today.

"Her father will be the one searching for her, and it's now your responsibility to make sure he never gets to her. Understand?"

"I'll protect her, Brianna, I promise."

I nodded my head, and she went about the task of loading the car, leaving me alone with Hope. There was so much I wanted to say, but I knew she was nowhere near understanding, and so I sat there gently rocking my baby to sleep. With every breath I took, I inhaled deeply her sweet baby scent, praying the memory of it could forever be stored in my brain.

"Mommy loves you so, so much, baby. Always remember that," I whispered, kissing the top of her head, fighting the tears that wanted to spring from my eyes.

Sooner than I liked, CJ was back and standing in front of me, waiting for me to hand her Hope. My heart had never known such anguish, but if I ever wanted more for my baby, then I had to act now.

"It's half a million dollars in the briefcase, and if anything happens, I want you to contact the Law Offices of Merril Lynch. After our wedding we had wills drawn up, so everything is straight."

"Wills?"

"Just take care of her, Casey," I said, reluctantly handing Hope over.

My ringing phone got my attention, so I didn't have to watch her walk out the door, but it wasn't who I hoped it would be. Going back into the office, I took the .45 out of the top drawer, checking to make sure it was loaded before tucking it into the back of my jeans and then headed for the car. Once I was behind the wheel of DJ's Bugatti, I programmed the address of my destination and prayed I'd make it in time to avoid absolute chaos.

"Call Evy," I said, catching sight of the blue Porsche cresting the hill in the opposite direction I was headed.

"Hello?"

"Evy, it's Bri. Have you heard from DJ?"

"No, not since he landed at Dulles Airport."

"How long ago was that?"

"About an hour ago, and he was on his way home from the airport. Why, what's wrong?"

"He's not answering his phone. I've been trying to call him since yesterday."

"Well, yesterday he was meeting with Ramona and all of her people, which kept him hella busy, and then he took CoCo to her mom's in Kentucky. I don't know why he wouldn't be answering right now."

"How's he travelling?" I asked, my worry shifting into almost blind fear.

"He's with Ramona and Bella in a limo. What the fuck is going on, Bri? And where are you?"

I didn't know where to begin explaining or even how much to say. I couldn't tip my hand until I knew what Devonte and Ms. Gladys had planned, but I could feel the walls of time closing in on me fast.

"I'm just worried, Evy, and I'm on my way to an important meeting. I need you to get ahold of DJ, ok?"

"I'm on it, and I'll have him call you immediately."

"Thanks, Evy," I replied, disconnecting and pushing the pedal of the Bugatti almost to the floor, needing to get to my destination A.S.A.P.!

There were a million thoughts racing through my mind, but I couldn't lock onto any single one long enough to find a solution to the problems. The one thing I didn't understand was why Tae picked now to come at us. Neither of us had done anything to provoke him. Shit, I'd even gone out of my way to make sure that "sighting" at the funeral was a distant memory.

Granted, I hadn't let him physically see Hope, but starting an all-out war and feeding frenzy wouldn't get him any closer to her. Did he really expect me to leave my husband and what we were building because he threatened me? The nigga was twisted if he thought there was a chance between me and him, so I didn't really understand what his end game was.

I knew I'd get a sneak peek at it now, though, as I cruised into the McDonald's parking lot and stopped next to Ms. Gladys. She was leaned against Tae's black BMW like she didn't have a care in the world, which pissed me straight the fuck off, because she obviously thought this shit was a game. I wasted no time stepping out of the car, making sure my t-shirt was concealing the gun. Her expression seemed to be guarded and somewhat unreadable, at least until I stepped around the car and she got a look at my bulging mid-section.

"Oh God, y-you're pregnant?" she asked.

"I damn sure ain't just fat, but you don't sound like you're about to congratulate me."

"That depends on who the father is."

"My husband is the father, of course," I replied, showing her the eleven-carat diamond DJ had picked out for me.

"Y-your h-husband," she stammered, her eyes widening like a junkie who had just taken a blast of hard.

"Yes, my husband, Ms. Gladys. Which is why I've come to ask you to broker a truce, if not for our sakes, then for that of your great grandkids. I don't know what's got Tae's panties in a bunch, but all we want is to be happy and done with the drama."

"If that's true, then why the fuck haven't you allowed him to see his daughter yet?"

"I was waiting for the right time, and I told you that! Shit has been hectic, and now you all are trying to add to the chaos with these bullshit stunts. Everybody knows my husband ain't no snitch. He was raised better than that."

"First of all, I don't know how long you expected us to wait to see Hope, or if there ever would've been a right time in your mind. Shit can't be too hectic if you found time to get married and fuck your baby daddy's brother enough to get pregnant!"

"Who I fuck and how often I choose to fuck them ain't neither of your business! And you act like I didn't send you pictures of Hope, because I didn't have to do that much!"

"Bri, what happened to you? When did you become that hood-bugger bitch who would keep a child away from its father?"

"Around the same time my child's father thought it was okay to execute helpless kids like we were at war in a third world country!"

"Devonte didn't kill those kids!"

"Just because he didn't pull the trigger don't mean that blood ain't on his hands."

This truth seemed to shut her up for a moment, which led me to believe she'd obviously confronted him since our last encounter at the funeral. She knew what it was like to raise a monster, so I didn't get how she couldn't understand my need to keep my daughter pure, which meant far away from Tae.

"Do you think DJ isn't capable of the same things? Do you think he doesn't have just as much blood on his hands, if not more?"

"I know exactly what DJ is capable of," I said softly, remembering the fatal morning in the hospital.

"If you do, then how can you say he's a better example for Hope than her father would be?"

"Well, one thing that comes to mind is DJ ain't always with the shit, unlike Tae, who's trying to get us all killed right now."

"That video doesn't have anything to do with you, Brianna."

"Are you really this fucking naïve? If that video gets out to the masses, they're not just gonna come for DJ. They'll come for everyone. Did you forget your family is known for one thing more than anything else? Revenge! Why would anyone take a chance on that? I mean, he's Devaughn Mitchell Jr! That's why you can't out that video out there, or the recording."

I expected more argument, but she just looked at me. I could see the wheels turning in her mind, and I thought she was weighing the options, but that wasn't it. Whomever's idea it was to make that video with Tae impersonating DJ didn't think it all the way through, and it was clear in her eyes reality was now hitting home.

"Brianna, you and Hope have to come with us. We can keep you safe."

"You can keep us safe by not going through with this fool-ass plan!" I said in frustration.

"No, baby," she said, shaking her head slowly.

"Then don't act like you give a fuck."

"No, you don't understand! The video is already out."

"W-what?" I asked, suddenly feeling weaker than I could ever remember.

"I tried to stop it, baby, but after the deadline passed—"

"W-who has seen this video?"

"Everyone."

"Who?" I screamed, tasting the bile rising in my throat and almost losing my battle not to throw up.

"All the people DJ is in business with."

My mind went blank as what she said was digested. I didn't know the particulars of my husband's business dealings, but I knew the type of money he was touching only came from seriously bad guys.

"Oh God," I moaned, holding my stomach.

"Are you ok?" she asked, rushing toward me. When she was in arm's reach, I pulled the .45 and stuck it in her face.

"Bri!"

"Shut up, bitch, and get in the trunk."

"Little girl, I don't know who—"

I didn't let her finish before I smacked her with the butt of the pistol and grabbed her by her hair, dragging her dazed and confused to the car. Once I had her in the trunk, I hopped back behind the wheel and fishtailed out of the parking lot.

"Call Evy," I ordered, tears clouding my vision as I swerved from lane to lane, racing a clock I couldn't see.

"I'm here, Bri."

"Did you find him?"

"No, he's still not picking up."

"Evy, you have to find him, now!"

"What's wrong, Bri?"

"Everything is wrong! Someone is trying to kill us."

Aryanna

Chapter Eighteen

DJ

"Drive this muthafucka!" I screamed, firing shots as fast as I could out the limo window at one of the two vans that had tried to box us in.

I could hear Bella letting her Ruger speak easy to the van on the other side of us, and despite the danger of the situation, I couldn't help but wonder when and where my baby sister had learned to handle herself like that. There was no time to voice this question, though. I was just thankful she had my back.

I still hadn't gotten a good look at who the fuck had ambushed us, because their faces were covered in ski masks, but the guns they were letting loose all had one thing in common: a black flag. They'd been waiting for us when we left the airport, and as soon as we'd hopped on the highway, all hell broke loose. None of it made sense! I wasn't beefing with nobody, and they wouldn't shoot first if this was intended to be a robbery or a kidnapping.

Nah, this was a hit, and we'd been exchanging gunfire for the last few miles, which meant whomever it was had more than a little determination.

"I'm out!" I yelled, tossing my .40 DE to the floor beside Ramona.

In one fluid motion she passed me an AR-15, and I had it out the window, barking and making lunch meat out of the driver, causing the van to flip.

"Bella, use this. It's got black talons in it," I said, tossing her the AR.

She made quick work of the other van, but I still wouldn't feel anything near relief until I was at home and in a position to get some answers.

"What the fuck was that about?" Ramona asked as I picked her up from the floor and put her back on the seat next to me.

"I have no clue. I'm not beefing with nobody right now,"

"Shit, you could've fucking fooled me, DJ! What have you done?"

"I didn't do nothing!"

"Muthafuckas don't try to knock your grape off your shoulders in broad fucking daylight for no reason, now start talking," she ordered.

"Mona, I'm telling you I haven't done shit. I been doing straight business across the board, and everybody is eating."

"Obviously somebody is an unsatisfied customer. Do you know who it is?"

"Nah, their faces were covered, and all I saw were black flags."

"Bella, what did you see, sweetheart?" she asked her.

"The same thing DJ did, but whoever is behind those black flags is black."

"Are you sure?" I asked.

"Positive."

"Okay, DJ, so who rocks black in this part of town?" Ramona asked.

I was only coming up with two options as I searched my brain, and I didn't like the idea of going to war against either. We were close enough to Maryland for it to be the Black Gorilla Family, but we were in Northern Virginia, which meant it could be the G.D.s. Pulling my phone out, I quickly dialed Deshana's number, getting all the way to the last digit before realizing my battery was dead.

"I need your phone," I said to Ramona.

Once I had it in hand, I called Deshana, because if anyone knew which gang it was, it would be her. And maybe she'd know what prompted the attack.

"Deshana, it's me."

"DJ, I've been trying to call you. We've got problems."

"My phone is dead, and you damn right we got problems!"

"So, you talked to DayDay?"

"No, why?"

"Because she got shot at, nigga! Why the fuck do you think I said we got problems?"

"Because I got shot at!"

"Wait, what?"

"Yeah, some niggas were lying in wait when me, Mona, and Bella got back from New York."

"Are Bella and Mona a'ight?"

"Yeah, we're good and going to the house to regroup, but what happened with DayDay?"

As she explained what happened in Texas, I couldn't believe what I was hearing. Them muthafuckas had balls going after my big sister like that, especially since she wasn't part of that street life. It was cool, though, because now they had to deal with me and Deshana.

"Was it the same muthafuckas that came for you?" Deshana asked.

"Nah, these niggas were black flaggin', that's why I'm calling you so you can tell me who's after me."

"Black flags, huh? Let me check on it, I'll make some calls from the plane."

"The plane? Where the fuck you going? Because now ain't the time for vacations!"

"No shit, fool. I gotta make a run out west really quick, and it wasn't exactly a request I could turn down."

I didn't like the sound of this shit at all. I had no idea what was going on with her and her people, but right now I needed my sister by my side, and damn some gang politics. I knew saying that to her right then would cause a fight, though, not to mention make her think I was incapable of ruling this empire.

"How long will you be out west?" I asked.

"Why is she going to the west coast right now?" Ramona asked.

"Let me talk to Ramona," Deshana said.

I passed her the phone before leaning into the front of the limo to tell the driver to get us to my house as fast as humanly possible. With the direction my business had taken, I'd had to upgrade my security options, and right then I wouldn't feel safe until I was on my property. Everything still wasn't making sense, though. The Mexican Mafia and another gang made a move against us, and that was supposed to be a coincidence? If I believed that, then I should've stayed in New York and tried to buy the damn Brooklyn Bridge.

"What did she say?" I asked once Ramona had disconnected the call.

"That she'd be back as soon as she could, and she's probably thinking the same thing we are."

"Which is?"

"That there's something serious going on, and there's a lot we're not seeing."

"What do you think it is?"

"I don't know, DJ. I don't know what exactly you've been into lately."

"I swear to you, Mona, I've been moving like I'm supposed to move."

"Well, we need to figure this shit out, and quick."

"Let me see your phone again."

When she gave it to me, I called the only person who might have some immediate answers. I didn't even hear the damn thing ring before I heard the Mad Hacker's voice.

"DJ?"

"Yeah, it's me."

"Oh God, DJ, we've got problems, big fucking problems!" he yelled, panicked.

"Calm down Evy. I'm not hurt, and neither is Sharday."

"DJ, I don't know what you're talking about, but it's so much worse than you know."

I'd known Evy for years, and he wasn't given to panic easily, nor did he exaggerate. Right then he sounded like he was face-to-face with certain death.

"Talk to me, Evy. What don't I know?"

"I'm sending you something you need to see and hear, and then you call me back."

"Evy, just tell—" I looked at the phone, realizing I was now talking to myself.

"What's going on?" Ramona asked.

"I don't know, but whatever it is, it's bad."

The vibrating phone alerted me to a video message waiting to be seen, and I clicked to open it. What I saw froze the blood in my veins.

"I-is this a joke?" I uttered aloud.

"What, DJ?" Ramona asked.

I couldn't respond immediately. I first had to hit the button to view it again while praying what I was seeing was someone's sick, twisted attempt at humor. It wasn't any funnier the second time around. In a daze, I passed the phone to Ramona and tried my best to process what I'd just seen, but it made absolutely no fucking sense.

The video was of a meeting in a lawyer's office with various people sitting around the table, and in the background there was some type of board with a number of different criminal organizations and it's suspected members. Then in walks a muthafucka who looked so much like me I had to search my memory for this meeting, but I knew it never took place because that shit just didn't look right.

"I don't understand, DJ," Ramona said, giving me a puzzled look.

"Me either. Play the recording to it."

As soon as she hit the buttons to bring up the sound, I knew the life I'd known was over, and this was a fresh hell I couldn't imagine. The audio began with introductions of the three clean-cut white dudes sitting at the table, who were representatives for the FBI, DEA and ATF. From there the ugly brunette with splotchy skin introduced herself as the team leader for the joint task force operation going after all organized crime across the country. Lastly, some blonde, fat bitch who said she was sitting in for my usual counselor brought my look-alike into the room.

The video lasted long enough for me to come into the room and agree to betray everyone I worked with in exchange for immunity from prosecution for the murder charge I was facing. It was a lie, but it was a damn convincing one. Ramona looked at me, and I stared right back at her, both of us knowing a 180-second video had just sentenced me to death.

"DJ."

"It's not me, Mona, I swear."

"Can you explain it, any part of it?"

"No. Give me the phone so I can call Evy back."

When she passed it to me, I noticed how bad my hands were shaking, and I had to try three times before I could hit the right buttons to call him back.

"Evy, what the fuck is this?" I asked as soon as he answered.

"I don't know. I don't know, but everyone you wouldn't want to see it has seen it. What are we gonna do?"

I was so far from knowing the answer to that question it rendered me speechless. I was in bed with the mob, the Columbians, the Mexicans, the Japanese, and virtually every street gang known, and if all of them had seen that video, then everyone wanted me silenced.

"Evy, tell me everything you know."

"I know that for the first time in history, everyone is working together, and there's a $500,000,000 bounty on your head. I'm still trying to find out where the video came from, but whoever did it has covered their tracks, so it's gonna take time."

"Have you put the word out to everyone, denying the video?"

"Of course, DJ, but you try telling some very paranoid people not to believe what they're seeing with their own eyes. Not to mention the fact you did beat the murder case for a public shooting."

"Do everything you can to prove that ain't me, Evy. We should be safe for the moment, because we just pulled through the main gates."

"I'm on it. Bri should be there in a couple minutes."

"Wait, where the fuck is Brianna?" I roared.

"The G.P.S. in your car shows her going to a McDonald's in Herndon, but she's on her way back to the house. Don't worry, I've been tracking her ever since she called me."

"Okay. I want you to run a complete diagnostic of my security here at the house A.S.A.P. and get back to me."

"I'm on it," he replied, hanging up.

"Does he have any ideas?" Ramona asked.

"He's working on it."

"Omertá must not be broken," Bella said, looking at me.

"Who are you, and what happened to my sweet, innocent little sister?"

"He hasn't broken Omertá, Isabella, someone is just trying to make it look that way," Ramona said.

The limo stopped in front of my house, and I hopped out to grab Ramona's wheelchair, my eyes constantly moving and scanning for any sign of a threat. Once I had her in the chair, we moved quickly to the house, my baby sister as intimidating as a Roman sentinel with the AR-15 clutched in her grip.

"CJ," I called out as we came through the door.

Only the loud echo of silence answered my call, giving my house an oddly cold feeling that hadn't been there before.

"Intercom on, page CJ to the living room, immediately."

As the message went out all across the house, I made my way to my office to begin serious damage control.

"I'm gonna see what I can find out, and you should call Deshana," Ramona advised.

Instantly my mind made the leap to where Ramona's had gone, knowing that in Deshana's world, she had no options except to be her brother's keeper.

"System online, code word Griselda. 3-D face time with Blanco," I ordered.

Most people thought Pablo Escobar was the undisputed king of drug dealing out of Columbia, but Griselda Blanco had been the one to make him what he was. She was ruthless and driven, which made her a different type of deadly. When I looked at Deshana, I could only compare her to Griselda, the godmother.

"What's up, DJ?" she asked.

"Do not get on that plane."

"What? Why not?"

"Listen to me, Deshana, it's not safe for you or JuJu. There's a video that supposedly shows me offering my cooperation against everybody we're in business with."

"What? DJ, what the fuck are you talking about?"

"I'm sending it to you now, but please do not get on that plane!"

I could see the pensive look on her face, but what lay beneath the surface told me exactly how real all of this was about to get. I saw fear in Deshana, and she feared nothing. I caught

Ramona's eye as she wheeled into my office and signaled for her to send the video to Deshana.

"It's coming now," I said.

Still she didn't utter a word, but merely nodded her head. I had no idea what was running through her mind right then, but I prayed it wasn't doubt, because if she didn't believe me, then nobody would. I held my breath when I heard the ping alerting her to an incoming message.

"I'll hit you back in a minute," she said, disconnecting before I could get a word in.

"You were right, DJ, it's bad," Ramona said coming around my desk and stopping in front of me.

"How bad?" I asked hesitantly.

"Bad enough my father is already in the air on his way from Italy."

"Why would he be coming?"

"Because he knows eventually someone is gonna kill you, and he knows I won't just let that happen."

Her words made my flesh crawl, but there was no room for lies right then.

"So, what do we do?" I asked.

"Do? There's nothing you can do. The wolves are coming."

Aryanna

Chapter Nineteen

In all the years I'd spent by my father's side learning, he'd never taught me how to face certain death. Maybe that was because he never gave up, or he just felt like no enemy he faced was worthy of killing him. Either way, I had to channel him if I hoped to get out of this in one piece.

"CJ's not anywhere in the house, and neither is Hope," Bella reported, coming into the office.

"What do you mean? Where's my daughter?"

"I was with you and Mom, so how would—"

"DJ! DJ!" Brianna yelled.

Jumping out of my chair, I rounded the desk and made it to my office door, where I collided with my visibly shaken wife.

"Baby, are you okay?" I asked, wrapping my arms around her, holding her close.

"Oh God, DJ, I was so scared. I thought something happened to you."

"I'm fine, babe, but where's Hope?"

"She's safe; she's with CJ."

"Where?"

"I didn't want to know, just in case."

"In case? How much do you know?"

Her tears were instantaneous, making me squeeze her tighter. I didn't want to offer her words or a promise I couldn't keep, and so I simply held her until the shaking in her body subsided a little.

"I'm so sorry, DJ, this was never supposed to happen."

"What do you mean?" I asked, pulling back so I could look down into her eyes.

The fear I saw hurt my heart, but it didn't stop the warning bells clanging loudly in my mind.

"I need you to promise to hear me out completely before you react or say anything, okay?"

"Okay," I replied hesitantly.

"First, I need to grab something," she said stepping out of my embrace and heading for the front door.

"Ramona, something's not right."

"I was starting to get the same feeling," she said, following me into the living room.

"What are you thinking?"

"I was thinking she's not a part of the business, so she should be completely blind to it, yet she had enough time and sense to get Hope out of here?"

I let those words bounce around the corners of my mind, but the feelings they generated were even less comforting than my original apprehension.

"Oh shit, is that who I think it is?" Ramona asked as Brianna came into the living room, gun in hand and at the base of my grandmother's skull.

"Brianna, what the fuck are you doing?"

"Baby, I can explain, but you have to hear me out."

"Okay, I'm listening."

"Sit down, you old bitch, and try not to bleed on my leather," Brianna said, pushing her down on the couch.

"You're only making it worse, Bri. He will come for me. Kidnapping me signed your death certificate," my grandmother warned.

"You've already done that, so shut up!" Brianna said, smacking her across the back of the head with the pistol.

"Brianna," I said, forcing her to look at me.

As soon as our eyes met, the tears started all over again. But as I looked closer, I saw the look in her eyes wasn't fear, it was regret.

"DJ, everything I did, every lie I told was for us. All I've ever wanted was for us to have a peaceful life and know what happiness was."

"What did you do Brianna?"

"I-I —"

Before she could finish, I heard the front door opening, and Deshana and JuJu walked into the living room.

"Thank God! Why didn't you call me back?" I asked, relieved to see them.

"Because I've been on the phone trying to figure out what the hell is going on," she replied, taking in the scene quickly, her eyes lingering on our grandmother.

"What's she doing here?" Deshana asked.

"Brianna was just getting ready to enlighten us," Ramona replied.

All eyes turned to my wife, and I saw that fear break back to the surface.

"Go ahead, Brianna, tell them your secrets," my grandmother taunted.

The tears steadily fell from Brianna's eyes like so many raindrops, but she managed to mouth the words *I love you* before taking a deep breath.

"DJ didn't make that video, and he didn't agree to betray anyone."

"How do you know any of this?" Ramona asked.

"Because I know that's not DJ in the video. It's Devonte."

"Bullshit, Devonte is dead," Deshana said.

"Have you listened to your voicemail messages, Deshana?" my grandmother asked.

I saw Deshana reaching for her phone, but my eyes remained focused on Brianna as I walked toward her. Standing right in front of her, I searched her eyes, willing my vision to penetrate to the very depths of her soul in search of the truth.

"Baby? Dead men don't make videos. So how long ago was it made, and how long have you known?" I asked.

I heard the familiar sound of a bullet being forced into the barrel of a gun, and I turned to see my sister taking aim at Brianna.

"DJ, move," she said.

"Hold up! You see she's pregnant, Deshana," I said stepping in front of my wife.

"Move, nigga! That muthafuckin' baby might not even be yours, considering her first baby daddy is still alive!"

"No, he ain't. I shot the nigga myself"

"What the fuck does that mean? I'm telling you he ain't dead," Deshana said, pressing buttons on her phone until she got what she wanted.

Suddenly Brianna's voice filled the air, along with my grandmother's. My heart stopped when the topic of who shot my father came up, but luckily Brianna had smoothly dodged that land mine. The rest of the conversation caused a familiar buzzing to begin in my ears as the pieces of the puzzle slid into place, allowing me to finally see the full picture. If the recorded phone call wasn't enough, the look on her face when I turned back toward her said it all.

"Y-you lied to me?"

"Baby, I did it for a good reason. If you would have known Devonte was still alive, there would've been another war, and I'm tired of all the fighting."

"That's bullshit, bitch, you just wanted to have your cake and eat it, too. DJ, move the fuck out the way so I can deal with this ho, and then her baby daddy," Deshana said.

"I got this, goddamn it!" I yelled.

But the truth was I had no idea what to do next. I believed Bri thought she was somehow doing the right thing, but too much had happened for apologies to be enough to fix this. There was no going back.

"Let me break it down for you, little bruh. Your sister, Sharday, is right now, at this very moment, being held hostage by niggas I thought were my homies. After she got shot at, I had my homies take her to safety in New Orleans, but my homies ain't my homies anymore. They want you dead, even if I have to kill you. And if that doesn't happen, they gonna kill her because Tae has put you in a fucked-up situation. He was only able to put you in that situation because of the two bitches in this room. Now, is your life worth theirs?"

How did I answer that question? My grandmother was a woman I didn't know, but I couldn't feel any remorse for her considering she'd obviously been helping Devonte. Sharday was my big sister, and I loved her beyond words, plus she was truly innocent in all of this. And then there was Brianna. Even knowing the hatred I should feel in that moment, I still felt a love stronger than any I'd ever expected to know. What we had went beyond words. It went beyond the imagination and understanding of anyone in this room except the beautiful woman standing before me.

From the moment we'd met, despite the circumstances, I'd felt a calm I didn't know I was yearning for. With her I'd found my balance, so without her what would I become? I had to find a way out of this for both of us, because life without her didn't hold the same appeal as it once did.

"Where is he, Bri?" I asked.

"I don't know, baby, I swear. That's why I took her."

"Where's your grandson, Gladys?" I asked her.

"Like I'd really tell you."

"One way or the other, we'll find him. The only question is how much pain you're willing to endure first. Before you answer that, you might want to digest the fact I am my father's son."

"Yeah, and I bet right now he wishes you were an abortion, you traitorous bastard."

"DJ, you need to move so I can rock this bitch," Deshana said impatiently.

"Baby, give me the gun," I whispered to Brianna.

"DJ, p-please. I'm so sorry."

"Trust me, babe. Give me the gun."

So much worry and doubt swam through her hazel eyes, but she reluctantly handed me the pistol.

"Stay behind me," I whispered, turning to face Deshana.

"I told you I got this, was I not clear? I'm not about to let you shoot my pregnant wife."

"Let me? Nigga, this bitch just betrayed our whole muthafuckin' family, and you think I need your permission to kill her? You better get your pussy-whipped ass out of the way!"

My response was to raise my gun until it was winking at Deshana, visibly flipping the safety off so she would know I wasn't fucking around.

"DJ!" Ramona said.

"Don't worry, Mona, that li'l nigga ain't got the balls to shoot me."

"He still doesn't need to be pointing a fucking gun at you! DJ, put it down and let's think this situation through."

"I'm not letting her die, Ramona, it's that simple. I don't care what she's done. I love her, and she's the mother to my children."

"And she's the reason we're all gonna fucking die, DJ! Don't you get it? My own hood turned on me, and everybody is gunning for us!"

"How is killing her gonna fix any of that?"

"It's a start, and it'll make me feel better. Now move, and that's the last time I'ma tell you."

I opened my mouth to speak, but the sound of glass breaking followed by metal skittering across marble froze the words in my throat.

"Grenade!" JuJu screamed.

I only had time to wrap myself around my wife and get her to the floor before the world shook beneath us. The blast was loud enough to make my ears ring, but there was no fire accompanying it, which meant it was a concussion grenade.

"We gotta move, babe," I told Brianna, pushing her toward my open office door.

I tried to get a look to see where everyone was, but the smoke was too thick. As soon as Brianna was across the threshold, I pulled the door shut and spun around in time to see a ghost step out of the fog. He was reaching for his beloved grandmother, but my shots forced him back into the hallway.

"Ramona!" I hollered.

"I'm here."

"Deshana!"

Her response came in the form of gunshots, but it was still music to my ears.

"I'ma kill you, nigga!"

I heard Devonte scream. Immediately I let rounds off in the direction his voice had come from, but it was a woman's scream that filled the air, causing terror to live in my heart.

"I got him, stop shooting," Bella said.

As the smoke cleared, I saw Ramona on the floor in front of the couch with a gun to my grandmother's temple, Bella had the AR-15 on Devonte, walking him into the living room, and Deshana was sitting on the floor with JuJu cradled in her arms. For a moment I thought I'd shot JuJu, but then I spotted the white girl bleeding out on the floor.

"Did you really think you'd make it out of here alive, nigga?" I asked.

"Didn't make a difference, because if I die, you die," he replied, smiling.

"Not likely, bruh, but you gave it your best shot. You can never be me, though."

"Oh, I don't wanna be you, but I can tell you wanna be me. Just because you can fuck a disloyal bitch don't mean you can be me, though."

"Aw, you sound just a little upset that both your baby mama and your daughter call me daddy," I replied, laughing and leveling my pistol to discourage the move his eyes were telegraphing.

"Let's see how long you keep that smile on your face after you're taken apart, piece by piece."

"Wishful thinking, Tae, but once I show everyone your dead body, the little video you shot will be irrelevant."

"Okay, but what about the fact you killed our father. Do you think your big sister is gonna forgive that?"

"Like she'd believe your lies."

"No, she wouldn't, but I've got a secret. My hacker is better than yours," he taunted.

I couldn't tell if he was bluffing or if it was even possible to recover what Evy had erased, but I was done talking. I pulled the trigger and hit him twice in the chest, loving the sight of him crumbling to the floor.

"Ramona, finish the old woman off," I said, turning back toward my office. What I saw froze me.

"Deshana, do not pull that trigger," I said as calmly as total fright would allow.

"Still not ready to make the hard decisions, huh DJ?" she asked, tears sliding with ease down her face. When I looked to my right, I saw JuJu laying in a puddle of blood, her eyes staring sightlessly at the ceiling.

"It's not a hard decision. She's carrying your nephew, and he's completely innocent in all this."

"None of us are innocent! Why is it so hard for you to see that?"

"My son is innocent. He's done nothing to you, Deshana."

"But what has his father done? Are you innocent, DJ?"

"Huh?"

"You fucking heard me!" she yelled, smacking Brianna with the pistol for emphasis.

"Innocent of what? What the fuck are you asking me?"

"Did you do it? Did you shoot dad?"

Even as I opened my mouth to speak, I realized no answer was gonna save both of us. I could see the madness dancing like flames in her eyes, and in that moment I knew she hadn't missed a word spoken between Brianna and my grandmother on that recording. Maybe she'd always had her suspicions.

"How could you think I'd do that? I loved our father."

"You know, I've played that night over and over again in my mind. You were consumed by hate and revenge, more than I've ever seen in anyone, including Dad. I know how much Dad loved his kids, so with him finding out the truth about Keyz, there's no way he would've killed Tae. And he wouldn't have let you kill him, either."

"And I accepted his decision."

"Did you? At first I thought you did, and so I disregarded the questions I had about the guns disappearing and Brianna's shakiness. But the gunshot wounds never made sense. If dad got hit while standing in front of you, then you should've never been hit the way you were. You may not be as good as I am with a gun, but you're not that slow, either."

"You're trippin'."

"Am I? Let's find out."

Before I could react, she'd stepped behind Brianna and I heard thunder roar. I'd expected her body to drop, but instead bright red formed at her shoulder and quickly soaked through her t-shirt while her screams pierced the air. Automatically my gun came up as I searched for a clear shot, but Deshana was smart enough to stay behind Brianna."

"Quick reflexes, junior. So, tell me again how Devonte shot you and Dad without you knocking his melon off."

"DJ," Ramona said. I didn't have to turn around to see the questioning look in her eyes.

My mind was racing and the pistol felt slippery in my grasp. The look in Brianna's eye was one of pleading, but all I could give her at this point was love. No matter what happened next, she would always know I loved her.

"My mother died before she had a chance to live, and for what? What was her crime aside from loving? Did she deserve to die just because she loved our father? No more than Brianna deserves to die for loving me or Tae. But what my mother did deserve was to have her death answered for. By any means necessary. One thing I learned very well from my father was that no matter how cold, revenge is a dish that must be served."

"What are you saying, DJ?" Ramona asked.

"I'm saying losing my mother didn't come without a cost, but for the first time I understand the cost might've been too high. So, it has to end now."

"You got that right, and it's gonna start with this bitch."

"Then you're next," I told her calmly.

It felt like time was standing still as I waited for Deshana to pull the trigger, but I never took my eyes off of Brianna. I prayed she could see all I didn't have time to say.

"I-It's okay, DJ, our love will live on," Brianna said through her tears.

"If you think I'm not gonna track your daughter down and end her, too, then you just don't know me," Deshana said, cocking the hammer on her pistol. In that moment, I knew what I had to do.

"Intercom on. Activate full lockdown, code word Caesar," I ordered.

Immediately the dome closed over the ceiling and eight-inch thick steel plates dropped all around the house, forcing the house into an almost blackout except for the emergency lights kicking on.

"DJ, what are you doing?" Brianna asked.

She knew what this lockdown meant and how it would play out, so my response was to give her a sad smile.

"I'm protecting our daughter," I replied, dropping my pistol.

"DJ, what the fuck is this?" Ramona asked, something resembling fear lacing her words.

"The end," I replied.

"The fuck you talkin' about, nigga? You better take this muthafucka off lockdown or I'ma blow this bitch's head off right now," Deshana threatened, once again putting her gun to my wife's head.

"I know you, Deshana, and you were never gonna let her live anyway. Your heart's too cold for that."

For once she didn't have a smartass comeback. She simply stared at me like she was trying to peep into my mind.

"DJ, whatever this is, you need to stop it, because you're scaring your sister," Ramona said.

"My sister doesn't scare that easy. And what this is, that's very simple to understand. Like Caesar, my reign has come to an end. But unlike Julius, I'm prepared to take all of Rome with me."

"W-what?" Ramona asked breathlessly.

I didn't get a chance to say anything else before the intercom came back on with the countdown.

Ten.

"DJ, stop it," Ramona said.

Nine.

"What happens when it gets to zero?" Bella asked.

Eight.

"He's bluffing," Deshana said.

Seven.

"Are you sure, DJ?" Brianna asked, looking at me.

Six.

"Yes, baby, I am. I love you."

Five.

"I love you, too, baby, more than anything."

Four.

"DJ!" Ramona screamed.

Three.

"Okay, DJ, goddamn it, I won't kill her," Deshana bargained.

Two.

"We dig many graves in the name of revenge."

One.

"And now we must fill them."

My smile was one of peace as the blast ripped through my house, and my last thought was that my pops would be proud.

I did it my way.

The End

<u>Coming Soon From Lock Down Publications</u>

THUGS CRY **III**

By **CA$H**

TORN BETWEEN TWO

By **Coffee**

LAST OF A DYING BREED

By **Jamaica**

GANGSTA SHYT **III**

By **CATO**

PUSH IT TO THE LIMIT **II**

By **Bre' Hayes**

BLOOD OF A BOSS **IV**

By **Askari**

BRIDE OF A HUSTLA

By **Destiny Skai**

WHEN A GOOD GIRL GOES BAD

By **Adrienne**

CHASIN' THIS PAPER

By **Qay Crockett**

<u>Available Now</u>

RESTRAINING ORDER **I & II**

By **CA$H & Coffee**

LOVE KNOWS NO BOUNDARIES **I, II & III**

By **Coffee**

LAY IT DOWN **I & II**

By **Jamaica**

PUSH IT TO THE LIMIT

By **Bre' Hayes**

BLOOD OF A BOSS **I, II & III**

By **Askari**

THE STREETS BLEED MURDER **I, II & III**

By **Jerry Jackson**

CUM FOR ME

An **LDP Erotica Collaboration**

A GANGSTER'S REVENGE **I, II & III**

By **Aryanna**

WHAT ABOUT US **I & II**

NEVER LOVE AGAIN

THUG ADDICTION

By **Kim Kaye**

THE KING CARTEL **I, II & III**

By **Frank Gresham**

THESE NIGGAS AIN'T LOYAL **I, II & III**

By **Nikki Tee**

GANGSTA SHYT **I &II**

By **CATO**

THE ULTIMATE BETRAYAL

By **Phoenix**

BROOKLYN ON LOCK **I & II**

By **Sonovia Alexander**

DON'T FU#K WITH MY HEART **I & II**

By **Linnea**

BOSS'N UP **I & II**

By **Royal Nicole**

I LOVE YOU TO DEATH

By Destiny J

<u>BOOKS BY LDP'S CEO, CA$H</u>

TRUST NO MAN

TRUST NO MAN 2

TRUST NO MAN 3

BONDED BY BLOOD

SHORTY GOT A THUG

A DIRTY SOUTH LOVE

THUGS CRY

THUGS CRY 2

TRUST NO BITCH

TRUST NO BITCH 2

TRUST NO BITCH 3

TIL MY CASKET DROPS

RESTRAINING ORDER

RESTRAINING ORDER 2

<u>Coming Soon</u>

TRUST NO BITCH (KIAM EYEZ' STORY)

THUGS CRY 3

BONDED BY BLOOD 2

IN LOVE WITH HIS GANGSTA

Made in the USA
Middletown, DE
30 March 2022